"I owe you a lot. You saved my life," he said

"I don't want you to remember it as a debt." Zoe let one slim hand travel experimentally over his shoulders.

"A debt is a debt," he murmured, intent on the course her hand was taking. Then with a groan he bent to her. Their mouths met and clung, and she felt helpless to deny the wild flood of response he aroused in her.

Her arms locked around his neck, which was smooth and strong like his shoulders. Fiercely she pressed against him, murmuring his name. As he kissed her eyes, her cheeks and her hair, she offered her mouth again with a complete lack of pretense or restraint.

Then his head jerked and he stopped. Tersely he said, "I think it's time you got some rest."

MARGARET PARGETER

storm cycle

Harlequin Books

TORONTO • NEW YORK • LOS ANGELES • LONDON
AMSTERDAM • PARIS • SYDNEY • HAMBURG
STOCKHOLM • ATHENS • TOKYO • MILAN

Harlequin Presents first edition November 1982
ISBN 0-373-10548-7

Original hardcover edition published in 1982
by Mills & Boon Limited

Printed in U.S.A.

CHAPTER ONE

ZOE was having a wonderful dream. She was out sailing. The sky was blue, the sea calm, and Macadam was with her. He had his arm around her and was smiling. There was something in his eyes she tried hard to see and in her eagerness to discover what it was she leaned too far over. The boat began rocking dangerously and she cried out.

Macadam's arm tightened painfully and his voice was impatient. 'Come on, Zoe, snap out of it, girl. Wake up!'

Zoe blinked, for a moment unable to comprehend where she was. Macadam was still with her, staring down at her, but he certainly wasn't smiling. The expression on his face was one of anger rather than pleasure, and they were in his office, not his boat, and he was shaking her, which would account for the rocking sensation.

'Macadam?' Drowsily she looked at him, her green eyes bemused.

After muttering something short and sharp beneath his breath, he snapped, 'What in heaven's name do you think you're doing here at this time of night, girl? Haven't I told you repeatedly not to come back to the office after you've finished work?'

After work—oh! Fully awake now, Zoe scrambled to her feet, her small face flushed. After she had finished checking the books she must have fallen asleep and started dreaming. 'You don't understand,' she murmured, her eyes widening anxiously. 'I helped Donald this afternoon, while you were away, and you did say you wanted the Renfrew account sorted out.'

'You didn't have to help Donald,' he said curtly, his arm going out to steady her as she stumbled. Roughly

he pulled her against him, one of his hands holding
her fair head against his shoulder while his other
tightened on her waist. 'You don't have to run each
time Donald lifts his little finger.'

It wasn't the first time Zoe had been in Macadam's
arms. Ever since she was small he had rescued her from
the scrapes she was always getting into, and as usual
she found his closeness comforting. When his long
fingers began gently massaging the back of her neck
she began feeling drowsy again. He was tall, his shoulders broad, and much as she disliked him he gave her
a great feeling of security.

She sighed deeply, strangely content until she heard
a sharp little cough behind them. Abruptly she
straightened to peer past Macadam's large frame. She
hadn't realised he had his girl-friend with him. Ursula
Findlay regarded her coldly, a look which Zoe returned
in full measure. If there was one person she couldn't
stand it was Ursula Findlay.

Sharply she tugged herself free of Macadam's sus-
taining arms. 'You can let go of me,' she said wilfully.
'I think I can manage without your assistance. I'm
tired, not tipsy.'

Macadam's mouth thinned and Ursula exclaimed
haughtily, 'You surely don't allow your workers to
speak to you like that, darling?'

Zoe knew a fleeting triumph when Macadam replied
shortly, 'Zoe's tired—as she says.'

Ursula frowned. 'I wish you'd get yourself a proper
secretary, Reece. I actually know of someone who
would suit you much better. After all, your boatyard's
no longer the small concern it used to be.'

'Which might speak for itself,' Macadam returned
dryly.

Zoe, making no sense of this whatsoever, felt bewildered, but only fools didn't realise when they were
being got at. How dared Ursula suggest she wasn't

good enough for Macadam? Well, Miss High and Mighty Findlay was about to discover some people fought back!

'Oh, Macadam,' she said sweetly, her smooth young face particularly innocent, 'Miss Vintis rang, just after you'd gone today. She said she was sorry about having to cancel your date for this evening, but she'll be delighted to dine with you tomorrow. Her mother gave her your message and she was sorry she'd missed you.' Disregarding the warning glitter in Macadam's dark blue eyes, she added recklessly, 'She hoped you'd been able to find someone else.'

As Zoe had expected, Ursula was immediately furious that she had been made a convenience of at the last minute. Before Macadam could get a word in, she lost her temper completely. She used language which Zoe considered no lady should use, not while she entertained any hopes of marrying the man she was addressing it to. If Ursula had kept her mouth shut and allowed a pathetic little tear to fall instead, Macadam might have reacted quite differently.

Zoe watched Ursula with pitying contempt. She had always suspected the girl had no brains, and this proved it. Macadam might have explained, if Ursula had given him half a chance, that his meetings with Miss Vintis were purely business, and arranged to suit her convenience, not his. Now he was so stiff with pride, Zoe knew he would never willingly explain anything. From the look on his face, Ursula's days were clearly numbered.

While feeling somewhat responsible, Zoe had no real regrets. If Macadam couldn't see for himself how most of his girl-friends were entirely unsuitable—well, someone had to! And it wasn't such an easy task. His apparent preference for beautiful but brainless women might have been easier to understand if he hadn't been so totally level-headed in other ways. Zoe found it very strange that such an arrogantly good-looking man of thirty-six should be so consistently blind when it came to women. Admittedly he appeared to have a kind of built-in radar device which enabled him to escape their final clutches, but Zoe derived little comfort from this. One day she feared he might succumb to the wiles of one of these dizzy, designing females, who would never tolerate the long hours he spent at the boatyard. It was for the sake of the boatyard, its future survival, she told herself firmly, that she felt compelled to keep such a close eye on Macadam's affairs.

Feeling quite pleased with her night's work, Zoe was complacent until she met Macadam's eyes again, and uncomfortably her heart gave a sudden lurch. He couldn't have guessed what she was up to. No, it wasn't possible. Of course he would be annoyed that she had been indiscreet, and she didn't doubt there would be repercussions, but when she explained that she had been too tired to realise what she was saying, and he had read her a little lecture—to which she needn't listen—then all would be forgiven.

He couldn't really do much else, could he? Zoe allowed herself to grow complacent again. She might not be a good secretary in the accepted sense, though she could spell and add and type neatly. It was her complete understanding of boatyard and boatbuilding jargon which made her indispensable. This and the ability to survive his temper! This was what the Ursulas of this world failed to understand.

'Let's get out of here,' Macadam said coldly, as Ursula was forced to pause for breath. Seconds later he was locking the door. 'I'll drop you off, Ursula.'

'Why don't you tell her she's dropped?' Zoe muttered cynically.

'What was that?' Macadam swung round on her.

'I said, she's stopped—to myself, Macadam.'

His blue eyes icy, he surveyed her narrowly. 'In the

car,' he said explosively, 'at once!'

Almost throwing her into the back seat, he helped Ursula more gently in beside him. 'I'll soon have you home.' His voice cooled politely.

'Oh, but Reece!' Ursula protested sharply, 'aren't we going on to Vicente's to dance?'

Vicente's was about the only place in the small, west coast of Scotland town, where people could eat, drink and dance to all hours. Zoe leaned forward, pricking her ears.

'Sorry,' Macadam replied, reeling the powerful car as if it was one of his racing boats at sea, 'I'm afraid I've changed my mind about dancing. I don't feel much like it now.'

Ursula, Zoe saw, cast him a quick glance. 'Don't be silly, darling,' she wheedled. 'Just because I was a little upset . . .'

'You had no need to be,' he retorted.

'You mean?' Ursula stared at him, her eyes wavering uncertainly.

'I mean, why don't women learn to think first and speak later, instead of the other way round?'

There was a short, tense silence, during which Ursula appeared to lose her temper again. 'If I jumped to the wrong conclusions,' she snapped back, 'it was entirely the fault of that impossible girl you insist on employing as your secretary!'

'She has a name.'

'I know all about her and her disreputable family,' Ursula blazed. 'Who doesn't?'

'Really?'

If Reece Macadam's smooth intonation held a hint of warning, Ursula obviously didn't hear it. 'Yes!' she all but spat. 'She has a name, but nothing to what I'd like to call her. She's a little bitch! She put ideas into my head about Miss Vintis. If it wasn't true what she said then she must have done it deliberately to make me angry. After all, no girl likes to feel she's been used as a last-minute substitute for someone else.'

'You're probably right,' Macadam said indifferently.

Outraged, Ursula cried shrilly, 'It's her you should be annoyed with, Reece, not me!'

The line of his jaw hardened. 'If you're talking about Zoe, I'll deal with her later.'

'You ought to sack her!' Ursula spluttered.

'I should?' Macadam's brows rose dryly.

Was he agreeing or asking a question? Zoe wondered, suddenly anxious.

'Everyone knows you let her get away with murder!' Ursula rounded off vindictively.

Macadam drew up sharply outside a large modern house. 'Goodbye, Ursula,' he said pointedly.

Ursula, after another furious glance at both of them, flounced out of the car, slamming the door.

Zoe stared after her, her startled glance quite unfeigned. Some people gave up very easily. 'She didn't expect that,' she said.

'Shut up!' tersely.

'I was only passing a remark.'

'You've no right to be passing anything,' he snapped.

'I've a right to be mad, surely,' Zoe muttered unwisely. 'Didn't you hear what she called me?'

'Wait till I get started!'

While Zoe shivered uneasily, he drove swiftly out of the town. He didn't take her straight home but along the coast road. The wind rose in squalls, there was a high tide running, the night was wild.

'Where are you going?' Zoe asked, alarmed. 'You know if I don't get in at a reasonable hour, Grandfather's furious.'

'That might be the least of your worries. I'll have a word with him.'

Uncertainly she frowned at him. Macadam was still in a temper. She decided to play it cool. 'I'm sure that won't be necessary. Not if you say what you have to say quickly and take me back?'

When he didn't say anything, either quickly or otherwise, her uneasiness increased. Macadam frequently took her home when they worked late, but he had never brought her this far before. As he drew off the road on top of a bleak, deserted headland, she clutched his arm, driven to ask,

'Why have you brought me here?'

'Why do you think?' His voice lashed her coldly.

Her hand dropped from his arm. 'Surely tomorrow would have done?'

'Not this time,' he retorted menacingly. 'This time I intend having my say without half my men rushing in to rescue you.'

'Why . . .' she began, her eyes widening indignantly.

'Don't try pleading innocence with me!' he rasped. 'Every time I raise my voice to you they're there, trumping up some unlikely excuse in order to rescue their helpless little chick. Well, for once,' he continued sarcastically, 'no one's going to get the chance of playing Sir Galahad!'

Alarm made her brash. 'You—you don't really mind about Miss Findlay, do you, Macadam?'

'That,' he replied, 'is none of your business.'

'I'm your secretary,' she protested.

'Which doesn't give you the right to run—or try to run—my private, personal life!'

How could he say that when she was often with him almost twenty-four hours of the day? Mutinously she said aloud, 'It's a different story, though, when I have to explain to your ex-girl-friends when they ring up that you're too busy to speak to them. You always ask me to do it. What's that if it's not part of your private, personal life?'

His blue eyes decidedly chilly, he ignored this. 'And so,' he said silkily, 'the list of my ex-girl-friends, as you choose to call them, grows, shall I say, mysteriously longer. Just how do you intend explaining what happened tonight? You know very well it's Miss Vintis who's been pushing the dinner dates, not me, and I only accepted in order to finalise the deal with her father over two new boats. You could have mentioned it, if you had to, without deliberately giving Ursula the wrong impression.'

'It was the way she was looking at me,' Zoe mumbled, as if this should explain everything.

'Why shouldn't she look at you anyway she likes?' he rapped. 'She was my guest.'

'Meaning?'

'I'm your boss.'

Zoe's cheeks flamed at the total lack of feeling in his voice. 'You may feel you need to emphasise the fact, but you couldn't do without me, Macadam.'

'Don't be too sure,' he rejoined softly, 'I might even be tempted to take up Ursula's offer. A new secretary could have other possibilities.'

'Don't you dare, Macadam!' she gasped. 'Don't you dare!'

'Don't you dare try and tell me what I may or may not do,' he countered, his eyes glacial.

They stared at each other warily, as they had been doing for years, ever since Zoe was a child and Macadam had first come to join his uncle at the boat-yard. She was nineteen now, but the years seemed to have made little difference. There was still the same antagonism between them, still the same spark which one wrong word could ignite into a raging conflagration.

'So you think I owe you an apology?' she murmured.

'That, or else . . .!' he threatened implacably.

'You wouldn't really send me away, Macadam?' Zoe's face paled and she shivered at the thought. She didn't want to leave Macadam.

Narrow-eyed, he regarded her silently. 'I might be

doing you a good turn, at that.' Soberly he paused again before adding, 'All you ever seem to think of is the boatyard and what goes on there. I'm not sure that it's healthy for a girl of your age. How old are you, Zoe?'

'Nineteen.'

'And never seen anything yet. Have you even had a boy-friend?'

'You would have known.'

'Not necessarily,' he said curtly. 'I'm abroad quite a bit and I take an occasional break. You could be up to anything while I'm away.'

'I usually tell you what I've been doing when you get back,' she reminded him. 'You know I have a full day at the office and spend most evenings at the boat-yard. I don't have much time for boy-friends.'

Macadam said dryly, 'You could make some time for other things, including boy-friends.'

'Do you think anyone would really fancy me?' she asked slowly.

'Any reason why not?' his glance travelled over her frostily, as if she had dared criticise something he had fashioned himself. 'You're too thin, but you have plenty of shape in the right places. Your skin is beautiful, so are your eyes, and your hair is thick and long and glossy. Your ...' he paused abruptly when he arrived at her mouth, taking in the soft, sensuous full-ness of it, which clearly threatened the untouched in-nocence of her face. His own tightened and he quickly transferred his interest to her nose.

'Do I have a smut on it?' Zoe asked somewhat aggressively, not at all sure she appreciated such an intimate surveillance.

'No,' he smiled, although it looked forced, 'it's very nice.'

'A bit silly.'

'I don't think so.' He ran a teasing finger lightly

down the slightly tilted tip of it. 'A little cheeky perhaps, but delightful.'

Feeling the pulse in her throat for the first time she could remember, Zoe jerked back. It beat uncomfortably fast. Never having been aware of it before, she felt nervous. 'You're making fun of me,' she accused him.

'Not entirely.'

Because she still felt distracted, she confessed without meaning to, 'Ian's asked me to see a film with him on Saturday night.'

'Graham?'

'Yes.' She looked out across the wind-tossed sea.

'Are you going?'

'I said I'd let him know.' The waves were breaking on the jagged rocks below, throwing foaming spray a mile high, towards a darkening sky.

Macadam was silent. Zoe dragged her gaze from the stormy ocean to glance at him. He turned his head and their eyes met. His were glittering strangely. 'Do you like Graham?' he asked.

'Yes,' she replied frankly. 'Everyone does.'

'Well, just watch it, Zoe,' he advised sharply. 'Graham has been around.'

'Most men have, according to Gran, but I can look after myself.'

His expression said he doubted this very much. 'What's Taggart going to say if you go?'

Zoe shrugged. 'I'll worry about that when the time comes. Grandfather isn't all that unreasonable, you know. If he thought something meant a lot to me he wouldn't stand in my way.'

'And Graham means a lot to you?'

'Not yet,' she replied cautiously.

'But he might?'

A little devil drove her on. 'Would you have any objections, Macadam?'

'Graham costs me a lot. I'd rather he concentrated on our new design. We have a lot of money sunk in it.'

'You feel I could distract him?'

'Possibly.' Macadam's voice was clipped.

Zoe's attention wandered again to the thundering surf. 'I think he's lonely.'

'Don't let pity swamp your better judgment, Zoe.'

'Maybe I'm lonely too,' she shrugged.

He frowned. 'Lonely for what?'

'I'm not sure,' she bit her lip. 'It's just a feeling I have.'

Impatiently he said, 'You're so young your feelings are bound to confuse you. It's all part of growing up.'

Moodily she stared at him, shaking her head. 'I don't expect you to know what's wrong with me, Macadam, but I thought you'd be more helpful than that. I seem to be changing somehow. It's not easy to explain, because I don't really understand myself.'

'You probably soon will,' he replied dryly. 'And I don't want you to be with Graham when you do discover what it's all about.'

Macadam was being enigmatical again. She hated it when he talked this way. Confused, she said, 'I'm sure Ian wouldn't harm me.'

'It depends what you mean by harm. I think he's too old for you.'

'He isn't thirty,' she protested, 'not as old as you.'

'What's that got to do with it?' he snapped. 'I don't happen to have questionable designs on you.'

'I never for a moment imagined you had!' Sulkily she tilted her chin, while wondering why she felt so depressed. Closely she scanned his hard face, the lean, tough body which had proved over and over again its limitless endurance at sea. Suddenly she was aware of a deep admiration which she felt bound, if only because of their old feuds, to hide from him. Yet he had taught her so much that if she had anything else to learn she would rather it was from him. Despite the way she constantly questioned his authority she had to admit he was nearly always right about most things.

As she became conscious of how intimately she was regarding him, her cheeks went pink and she dragged her eyes away from his. A peculiar kind of tension was mounting rapidly between them, driving her to say hurriedly, 'You'd better take me home. It's getting late. Grandfather . . .?'

He nodded curtly, with a last quick glance at her averted face. 'He's another feature in your life that will have to change.'

As he drove her back to the straggling town, then through it to where her grandparents lived, they were both silent, busy with their own thoughts. Outside the modest cottage, overlooking the sea, the car had no sooner stopped than her grandfather was there, confronting them.

'A fine time of night this is to be coming home!' He glared from Zoe to Reece Macadam angrily. 'I went to the yard, but you weren't there. Where've you been, Zoe?'

Taggart Kerr, Zoe's grandfather, was a huge man with flowing white hair and a beard to match and a pair of snapping black eyes. His temper was renowned throughout the district and most people were slightly afraid of him. Only Macadam stood up to him, but Zoe doubted if Macadam had ever been afraid of anything or anyone in his life.

He said now. 'It's my fault, Taggart. I kept Zoe talking.'

'What about?' Taggart glowered, as Macadam went casually to help Zoe out. He watched suspiciously as Macadam kept his arm around the girl. He didn't know Macadam left it there because he could feel Zoe shaking. 'What about, man?' Taggart repeated.

Macadam looked him straight in the eye. 'Nothing

that need concern you,' he replied evenly.

'Don't tell me my granddaughter is no concern of mine!' Taggart exploded. 'I demand an explanation!'

Zoe shrank closer to Macadam, drawing comfort from his strength as she glanced at her grandfather nervously. His temper was rising. Macadam had a temper, too, and she wanted to avoid a head-on clash between them. They were liable to wake half the town, if they once got started.

'There's no explanation to give, Grandfather,' she intervened quickly. 'I was working late and fell asleep. Macadam was passing the office with Miss Findlay and came to investigate. He brought me home, that's all.'

Taggart's great bushy brows drove together, but he appeared partly mollified with the half-truths of Zoe's brief statement. 'You ought to get your locks changed, Reece, and refuse to give her a key. You're her employer, you shouldn't allow her to stay there until all hours. She's beginning to grow up and there'll be gossip.'

Macadam's eyes glinted and his hold on Zoe tightened. 'What sort of gossip had you in mind, Taggart?' he asked silkily.

The old man, still almost as steel-nerved as the man who faced him and without discretion when it came to his beloved granddaughter, bellowed, 'About you and her, man! People will talk about anything, given half a chance.'

'Only if they have minds like yours,' Macadam retorted furiously. 'The first man I hear saying anything about Zoe won't know what hit him, and that includes yourself!'

Zoe felt something startling leap through her, but had no time to decipher what it was. 'Please, Macadam,' she said sharply, pushing him away when she wanted to cling to him, 'thanks for the lift, but don't say anything more. I don't want you threatening my grandfather because of me.'

'I'd do more than threaten,' he muttered danger-ously, his breath suddenly warm on her face. Frowning, he gently touched her pale cheeks. 'Are you sure you'll be all right?'

Immediately suspecting he was taunting Taggart indirectly, she jerked back. 'Of course I'll be all right. I can fight my own battles.'

'Some of them,' he conceded, getting in his car. 'Fortunately there aren't many men around like your grandfather.'

Before Taggart could recover sufficiently from such an insult to reply, he was gone, leaving them both star-ing after him, if with very different expressions on their faces.

'I don't want you coming home at this hour with Reece Macadam again.' As if hoping to regain what little face he had lost, Taggart lost no time in turning on Zoe as soon as the cottage door closed behind them. 'Did you hear what he said to me, the way he spoke to me? If his uncle had still been alive—God rest his soul, I would have gone immediately and had a word with him!'

Zoe, retrieving her composure, merely shrugged. 'It's only after eleven, for goodness' sake! And if you don't be quiet you'll have Gran down.'

'At least she's a good woman, quiet, respectable and God-fearing, not like some!'

'Oh, Grandfather,' Zoe glanced at him, grinning wryly, 'I'm not that far beyond hope, surely?'

'I have to watch you because of your father,' Taggart retorted sulkily.

Zoe sighed helplessly. She could barely remember her father, since she had only been a few years old when her parents had both died in an accident. 'You talk about being God-fearing,' she muttered, 'yet surely no Christian would be forever remembering how his son displeased him. It wasn't as if my father had committed any crime!'

'No crime!' Taggart's voice rose wrathfully. 'Didn't I do without to give him a good education, and what did he do? He married a foreign student as soon as he got his degree, instead of coming back here to support your grandmother and me in our old age.'

'You know I'm sorry about that,' said Zoe, 'but it's not as if you've ever had to do without.'

'On top of that,' continued Taggart, as if Zoe hadn't spoken, 'your parents gave you your outlandish name, which we've all had to live with.'

Zoe, in fact, loved her name, but she hoped her grandfather would never discover it was the Greek name for life. Gran knew, but they had a pact not to tell him, as they feared it would hurt him too much. While he might pretend not to, Taggart had practically worshipped his son, his only child.

Zoe's mother, a Greek orphan, had been rejected by the distant cousin who was her guardian, after she had married a penniless Scotsman. Taggart Kerr had washed his hands of his son, too, so that the first few years of Zoe's life had been spent in the south of England, where her clever parents had both taught at a famous university. It wasn't until after her parents were killed that Zoe met her Scottish relations for the first time.

At seven, she had delighted and comforted a sorrowing Taggart by showing an immediate understanding of boats. She had told him, in her rather precocious manner, which had confused her grandparents at first, how her father had owned a small boat on the Thames and had taken her sailing from almost the day she was born. Taggart's delight had increased when she had formed a remarkable affinity with the boatyard where he had worked all his life. Every chance Zoe had got she had been there with him, soaking up knowledge like a sponge, over the years developing an expertise which astonished him.

Reece Macadam's uncle, Farquhar McNeill, was a hard man with little time for children, but he had tolerated Zoe, liking her spirit. When he died he left her a hundred pounds. He hadn't been married and had left everything else he possessed to his nephew.

Farquhar's sister, Reece's mother, had married the son of a rich Edinburgh family. Zoe had overheard him talking to her grandfather one day.

'They didn't think Fiona good enough. I imagine their fine feathers will be ruffled again when they discover her son is joining me.'

'As long as the joke doesn't rebound on yourself, Farquhar,' Taggart had warned sourly. 'I wouldn't like to see any young upstart wreck a business you've taken years to build.'

Zoe hadn't known what they were on about, but Gran had explained. Casting a quick glance at Taggart, she said quietly.

'Farquhar's nephew, Reece Macadam, is very keen to come here and learn everything about boats. He wants to build them and repair them, you see. He's a very nice young man, I believe, with a good education.'

'If it's done him as much good as it did Angus,' Taggart grunted, 'he'd be better off without it.'

Gran had been a teacher before she married Taggart and it had been she who had insisted that their son Angus go to university—something Taggart didn't allow her to forget.

'He doesn't mean anything,' she had often told Zoe. 'It's just when the bitterness comes over him that he can't help himself.'

From practically the first day he arrived, Reece Macadam had made changes at the boatyard. He was a tall, broad young man, whose air of terse authority made him seem older than his twenty-four years. Zoe had been barely nine. As time went by Reece turned what had been a modest little business into an extremely substantial enterprise. He achieved what his uncle proudly liked to call miracles, but not without some dissent from his uncle's right-hand man, Taggart Kerr.

Taggart had fought Macadam almost every inch of the way, those first years, before he was ready to admit grudgingly that the younger man knew what he was doing. Zoe remembered their many battles, with her grandfather's booming bellows heard halfway over town, and Macadam's clipped, uncompromising replies. Macadam usually managed to control his own not unformidable temper, but occasionally he wasn't above losing it.

Zoe recalled one incident in particular, because it marked the beginning of the antagonism which still existed between Macadam and herself. That day Macadam had been furious. Taggart had done something quite contrary to his orders and he demanded an explanation. When Taggart, a huge, Biblical figure, with his flowing white locks, began bellowing, Reece Macadam had shouted him down. Language had been used which had coloured the air, making even the raucous seagulls fly off.

Zoe had been told by her grandmother never to interfere, but unable to stand it any longer, she had flung herself fiercely at Macadam, her small face red with indignation, ordering him wildly to stop bullying her grandfather.

Macadam with his superior strength had thrust her aside, without even sparing her a second glance. 'Can't you leave that damned brat of yours at home for a change, Kerr?' he'd snapped.

'Don't you bloody well swear at me, Macadam!' Zoe had shouted.

He had picked her up then, by the scruff of her neck, and thrown her over his knee. With the entire boatyard looking on, he had laid into her, ignoring her loud screams, while Taggart had practically danced with rage and threatened everything, including his resignation.

When he had let her go Zoe had quietly hated him. She wasn't sure that she still hated him, but from that day on it had been Macadam. No one could ever remember her calling him anything else. And, strangely, she was the only one ever allowed to call him Macadam. To the men he was either Reece or Mr Macadam, according to their age and length of employment. The men accepted that Zoe addressed the boss differently, it was doubtful if now they ever gave it a thought. Neither had Zoe, at least, not until recently, when, to her astonishment, one afternoon, she had found herself staring after him as he left the office, whispering his Christian name experimentally, as though she had an irresistible urge to try it out.

As a faint flush coloured her pale cheeks, Taggart asked suspiciously what she was dreaming about. Suddenly coming back to earth, she apologised quickly.

'I'm sorry if you've been anxious, Grandfather, but let's not quarrel any more,' she pleaded. 'I promise I'll try to let you know if I'm going to be late again. Now how about a cup of tea?'

'You'd better put a wee drop of something in mine.' Taggart's pious tones suggested she had put him through a far greater ordeal than she realised.

With a wry smile, Zoe departed to the kitchen and plugged in the kettle.

CHAPTER TWO

Taggart went to bed still muttering, and Zoe followed suit. Next morning she was at the office early. Macadam was already there, talking to Ian Graham. They had their heads together over a drawing board in the design department.

'Good morning,' she called as she went past the door.

'Oh, hello, Zoe,' from Ian. 'See you later.'

Nothing from Macadam but a dark nod. She hoped it wasn't an indication of his mood for the rest of the day.

She continued upstairs to the main office. The cleaners had been through, leaving everything neat and spotless. After hanging up her coat she went and opened the windows to get rid of the smell of disinfectant. Mrs Scott must think they were all suffering from some contagious disease, the way she used it!

The mail hadn't arrived yet, but there was plenty to be getting on with. Despite this Zoe lingered by the last window she opened. The morning sunshine beckoned as it played on the waters of the harbour. Wistfully she gazed down on it. March in the Western Highlands could be a very stormy month and during a spell of fine weather like this it suddenly seemed a crime to be stuck indoors.

She glanced across to where some men were working on the boats moored to the wharfs. There was the sound of machines starting up from the big sheds on the shingle above the high water mark. Zoe sighed with envy, wishing she could be out there with them.

Resolutely she turned her back on temptation to sit

down at her desk. Carefully she removed the cover
from her typewriter and inserted a clean sheet of paper.
If Macadam was out of temper it would never do for
him to come and catch her idling!

Sometimes she wondered what she was doing here.
It had been Macadam who had insisted she train as a
secretary after she had disagreed with Gran about going
to university. It had nothing to do with her dad, she
had argued, she just didn't feel cut out for an academic
career.

'I'd rather work at the boatyard, like Grandfather,'
she said.

'Call it sex discrimination or what you like,' Janet
had declared, 'but you know Mr Macadam would
never employ you.'

'Grandfather's retiring soon. There'll be a vacancy.'

'No!' said Macadam, when she approached him.
'Definitely not.'

'What shall I do, then?' she had glared at him, her
manner suggesting he had deprived her of the only job
she was ever likely to get.

'Take that self-pitying expression off your face for a
start,' he had snapped.

'I—I know as much about boats as any of your men,'
she had spluttered, outraged.

'So you do,' he admitted, doing one of his quick
turnabouts which never failed to confuse her. 'I tell
you what, Zoe Kerr, go and get some clerical training
and I'll give you a job. A trial run, anyway, to see if
you suit me.'

She hadn't altogether trusted the gleam in his eye,
the smoothness of his voice. She had had an uneasy
suspicion that he believed after two years she would
no longer want to work for him. She had endured the
secretarial college for six months, when her grandfather
told her Reece had had a row with his latest secretary.
Immediately she heard, Zoe rushed to confront him.

'You promised!' she cried.

'You haven't finished your training yet,' he rapped back.

'I don't want to,' she replied.

'I must be mad,' Macadam sighed, 'but if you think working for me will leave you unlimited time for messing around with boats, then you'd better think again.'

Nevertheless, Zoe had managed to survive. Not only that, she had been a success. While she mightn't be brilliant, she was highly intelligent. She could do anything with figures and never used a dictionary, or needed to, and anything a prospective customer wanted to know about the boat he was buying, if Macadam wasn't there, she could tell them. If she had one bad fault it was her habit of disappearing to help one of the men. It was fortunate that Macadam always knew where to find her.

The door opened furtively and Ian stole in. Putting an arm round Zoe's shoulders, he kissed her lightly on the cheek. 'And how's my lovely girl this morning?' he smiled.

'Without time to provide you with an amusing half hour!' Macadam's voice hit them from behind.

Ian flushed and went away.

'Damn you, Macadam,' Zoe gasped, 'he wasn't doing any harm!'

'That's a matter of opinion,' Macadam snapped, 'and don't use language like that in here.'

'I've heard worse.'

'So have I. When you were eight, or was it nine, and you suffered for it. I don't want to have to put you over my knee again.'

'Then you'll have to think of something else,' Zoe taunted rashly.

'That shouldn't be too difficult,' His eyes glinted. 'Perhaps you prefer the kind of punishment Graham was dishing out?'

Zoe blinked. 'He was only kissing me . . .'

'You didn't mention that you'd got as far as that!'

She flushed. It was the first time Ian had, but she wouldn't tell Macadam. Why should she? 'I'm sorry,' she said sedately.

Macadam disappeared into his office, slamming the door.

Ten minutes later Zoe followed.

'Can't you knock or buzz to say you're coming?' Macadam snarled. 'You've simply no idea of the proper way of going on, nor are you willing to learn.'

'I usually knock or ring to ask if it's all right,' she defended herself, meeting Macadam's arctic blue eyes. 'If you're suffering from a broken heart, this morning,' she added flippantly, 'the message I have might cheer you up.'

'I won't warn you again, Zoe,' he said grimly. 'And don't bother to apologise. I dislike insincerity as much as anyone. Come on, then,' he stretched back in his chair, 'what's this great news flash that's going to change my life?'

Goodness, she'd be lucky to get out of here alive! Taking a deep breath, she contrived to sweeten her voice. 'Miss Findlay rang to say she's giving a party—or her mother is, tomorrow night, and you're invited.'

Dead silence. The office walls might have revealed more than Macadam's face, which was absolutely expressionless. Rather desperately, Zoe tried again. 'Then Miss Vintis. She's coming along at eleven with her father and brother. They—the father and brother, I gather—arrived unexpectedly last night and would like to meet you. She suggested eleven and asked me to ring her back if it wasn't all right. Apparently her brother is keen to check you have exactly what he wants before coming to a final decision.'

'That's all I need!' Macadam exclaimed. 'Someone

who's probably never sailed before telling me how to run my own business.'

'It mightn't come to that,' Zoe said soothingly.

'I haven't your faith in human nature,' he retorted.

She shrugged and left him, hearing the mail come in.

'You'd better get in touch with Miss Vintis and tell her I'll be delighted to see them,' Macadam said with heavy sarcasm, as she went out.

When Zoe returned with the sorted mail and her notepad, he asked laconically, 'How would you like to go to the Findlay party, Zoe?'

'Not particularly,' she said.

'Well, you're going,' he informed her, 'and that's an order.'

She laid the mail down on his desk with an uncertain frown. 'You'd better think again, hadn't you?' she lifted her eyes to meet his hooded ones. 'A, I don't have a suitable dress. B, Ian's asked me out on Saturday night, and C, the Findlays didn't invite me. They may not like it.'

'A,' he retorted testily, 'you can buy a dress, I'll give you the money. B, you told me you hadn't given Graham a definite answer. And as for C, the Findlays can lump it if they don't like it, but you can take it from me there'll be no objections.'

'How can you possibly know that? Macadam,' she asked anxiously, 'what makes you think I'll be accepted?'

'If for no other reason than that you'll be with me,' he replied dryly, 'But you're as good as they are any day. Jack Findlay might happen to be related to a title, but he's no snob.'

That Zoe couldn't deny, but he had an extremely snooty wife and daughter.

'You wouldn't be trying to find a plausible excuse, would you?' he snapped. 'It's not often I ask you to do anything for me away from the office.'

'And sailing,' she tacked on automatically, thinking of the long hours at sea when she'd crewed for him, helping him test new ideas and equipment.

'You can't make me believe you're complaining about that?' Macadam jeered softly.

'I still don't know why you're so keen to go to this party,' she murmured. 'After all, your romance is over.'

'Is it?' He stared at her coldly. 'If it is, then you could be partly responsible.'

Zoe went white and knew he must be aware of it. 'You mean you're going to take me there in order to make me pay for my sins? To make Ursula jealous?'

'No,' he said shortly, 'you're wide of the mark, as usual, but I haven't time to explain.'

Startled, she glanced at the clock. 'Oh, gosh,' she exclaimed childishly, 'they'll be here soon and I haven't even got the coffee on!'

'No need for panic!' He reached out impatiently, pushing the mail out of sight in a drawer. 'That will have to wait, and for heaven's sake don't trip over with the coffee or spill someone's whisky on the floor. Oh, and have a clean pad ready, so if they do make up their minds about what they want, you don't get their order muddled up with someone else's.'

'I do know that much!' Zoe bristled. How unfair could you get! 'I've never made a mistake like that all the time I've been working for you. Why should you think I'm going to do so now?'

'Well, don't let's argue about it,' he retorted, without apology. 'Just remember what I've told you—and don't forget to look pleasant.'

Driven to insolence, she said angrily, 'I wonder if you know the meaning of the word?'

'Oh, get out!' he snapped, leaving his chair to turn his back on her as he walked across the room and began rummaging in a cupboard.

Zoe spent the next few minutes calming down and seeing to the coffee. As she set a tray with four cups and checked their supply of clean glasses, she wondered how she was going to explain to Ian about Saturday. She would much rather have gone sailing on her own than out with either of them. She couldn't very well tell Ian this, though, as he had done nothing to deserve such bluntness. Nor did she care to confess to him that Macadam had asked her out, then made it an order when she had refused. She could, of course, still refuse to go with Macadam, she doubted if he would sack her, but an odd urgency was rapidly getting the better of her. If she didn't go she wouldn't know what was going on, and she couldn't bear to wait until some later date to discover if he and Ursula were friends again. No, she decided, her mind made up, she would go and remain glued to his side, whether he liked it or not!

She hoped Mr Vintis and his family wouldn't be late. In the mood Macadam was in he was quite liable to disappear, leaving Ian or her to do the negotiating. It wouldn't be the first time.

They were on time. Mr Vintis wrote highly successful novels which were often made into films. Zoe had read somewhere that many writers had no idea of time, but Charles Vintis was clearly a man of method. She glanced with interest at his daughter, whom she had spoken to on the telephone but never met. They were a London family who, six months ago, had bought a house in the district and intended living here for the greater part of each year.

From her voice, Zoe had gathered the impression that Miss Vintis was older and plain. Older she might be, but never plain. She was beautiful, with a nice open, laughing face. Zoe gazed at her in dismay. Her brother might have been a few years younger, around thirty or so. He looked all set to take over the world.

She admired his air of supreme confidence while suspecting Macadam mightn't.

'Mr Macadam is expecting you,' she smiled formally. Recalling his lecture on how a proper secretary should go on, she rang through to make sure he was ready to receive them. He was. 'If you'll just come this way, please?' She stood up, still smiling formally.

Reece, however, was at the door before she reached it. 'Is he your boss?' Freddy Vintis asked in a low tone.

She nodded primly, aware of Reece's glance flicking her coldly. 'I'll be in touch.' Freddy Vintis leaned outrageously near her ear.

'See to the coffee, Miss Kerr, when you have a moment, please,' Reece emphasised the "when" sarcastically, and Zoe flushed.

Silently she fumed as she switched off the percolator, not caring if the coffee was properly ready or not. Macadam couldn't expect perfection when he so clearly indicated she fell far short of it!

When she went through with the coffee he was explaining details she knew by heart but never tired of hearing. Macadam had a way of talking about boats which never failed to grip her attention. He could make even a rowing boat sound something special.

Freddy Vintis jumped up, taking the tray from her. He had manners, as well as everything else, she mused, suspecting, as her eyes met a pair of steely blue ones, that Macadam had read her thoughts exactly.

As she poured coffee, Freddy Vintis hovered, never taking his eyes from her face. Obviously with a view to impressing her, he said loudly, 'I was just about to tell your boss, Miss Kerr, that I want something fast, with the most powerful engine you've got—or can get. I can't stand anything that's slow.'

Macadam interrupted politely but coldly. 'The careful choice of an engine is the only way to obtain maximum results from a boat. A racer can actually be slower with more powerful engines astern. I'd advise you not to be too ambitious to begin with, Mr Vintis. The sea, especially the coastal waters around here, calls for some experience and careful navigation.'

Freddy seemed less then impressed. 'Oh, I'll soon get the hang of it, Macadam,' he grinned airily. 'I've been reading books.'

'All very commendable,' Macadam agreed flatly. 'I read books on the subject and wrote two myself. But, years ago, practical experience taught me that there's a world of difference between classroom navigation and doing it out there.'

'Sure, you're probably right,' Freddy laughed, 'but that's no problem. I'll take somebody with me, the first once or twice. Miss Kerr, for instance,' he turned back to Zoe, his handsome face still wreathed in smiles, 'I bet you'd be willing to come with me and show me a thing or two?'

Later Macadam told her grimly, 'If you dare go out with that young fool I'll have your head examined!'

Zoe glanced up from rows of figures which were dancing crazily before her on a page. For the first time she couldn't make sense of them. She had been here in her own office answering the telephone when he had shown the Vintises out. Father and son had gone first, while Macadam had followed with Carol Vintis, steering her lightly, his hand on her waist. Suddenly Zoe had felt ill. Not another! She didn't think she could stand it. A terrible pain had lanced through her heart, making her wince.

Lowering her eyes quickly, for fear he might read what was in them, she muttered tightly, 'I didn't take his suggestion all that seriously.'

Looking anything but satisfied, Macadam retorted, 'He will undoubtedly kill himself. A pity—maybe?'

Zoe shrugged. 'You did your best to straighten him

out, so I shouldn't let him trouble you.'

'I'd never encourage suicide.'

'You could always pass on a few more tips when you dine with his sister.'

'My, Grandmama, what sharp ears you have,' he quipped tersely.

Zoe flushed angrily. 'When she asked you if tonight's arrangements still stood, she didn't bother to lower her voice, nor did you look particularly reluctant. Why don't you take her to Miss Findlay's party on Saturday instead of me?'

Macadam's mouth tightened, his glance smouldering over Zoe's pink face. 'I asked you, and I'd rather take you than anyone else.'

'I don't have to believe it.'

'I'd advise you to.' He came nearer, standing so close she could see the black rims around the pupils of his amazing blue eyes. 'Believe me, Zoe, there's a side to me you've never seen yet, so don't push me too far.'

Another side? She was familiar with his anger, being frequently subjected to it. His hardness she accepted, because it was the kind of toughness a man needed to cope with the harsher elements involved in work such as his. The strength often required to survive at sea was bound, in time, to affect a man's whole personality. She had also, on rare occasions, known his gentleness, so this other side he hinted at could only be sexual.

Shivering, as her pulses quickened alarmingly, she said, 'You might enjoy shocking me, Macadam, but I don't think you'd ever actually hurt me.'

'One day I may have to.'

He was staring, each word bitten off, and while Zoe couldn't read the look in his eyes, she felt her nerves flinch then tighten with a strange excitement. It was like being hurtled heavenwards, with no ability to resist the forces sweeping her there. Into the skies she went, helpless to fight the turbulent emotions which seemed to be emanating directly from him. All around her were clouds, black and terrifying, ringed with fire, lines she dared not cross. Yet the clouds beckoned treacherously, so incredibly soft that she wanted to.

'Macadam!' she gasped faintly, her trembling lips parting incredulously.

'Why not try calling me Reece?' he suggested, his eyes still hard on her face. 'It might make things easier.'

Something in his voice jerked Zoe to her senses. She tried to grasp what it was, but before she could it was gone. As though coming out of a trance, she blinked, shaking her head. 'I don't know if I could,' she whispered.

'Leave it,' he said expressionlessly. 'One day you might not find it so difficult.'

'You know I like to please you,' she found herself pleading, 'although it may not always be obvious.'

He smiled wryly at that. 'The understatement of the year.'

'Sometimes you make it difficult,' she defended herself indignantly.

This time he merely raised dark brows as he turned from her to stare out of the window. 'You know what I'd like to do? I'd like to take the ketch and go sailing. Somewhere really rough.'

Those sort of conditions demanded a man's full concentration, with no time to think of anything else. Why should Macadam want to forget everything? He had a good life here, hadn't he, among the islands. It must be almost as good as a man could get.

'Alone?' she asked.

'No—with you.'

'Because I don't get in the way?'

He glanced at her quickly. 'Forget it,' he shrugged. 'We've too much to do. The business would soon collapse if we all took days off whenever we felt like it.'

'It would be super, though!' Her eyes danced.

'The thought of a day's sailing always excites you, doesn't it, Zoe?' he sighed with a hint of impatience. 'Perhaps it's time you developed some enthusiasm for—other things.'

Her face sobered warily. He sounded depressed, but it probably wasn't her fault. 'It's not fair,' she said, 'to take it out on me, because you're still upset about Ursula.'

'You're probably right,' he agreed, his eyes glinting mockingly. 'Perhaps Miss Vintis will help to heal my broken heart tonight?'

Zoe's throat suddenly hurt. 'I didn't think you would need to take her out now.'

'Well,' his mouth relaxed slightly, 'there certainly won't be the same necessity to discuss business, but, as you have yet to discover, there are other things.'

Fear and rage drove Zoe from her seat to confront him. Infuriated, she gazed up at him. 'You can't be thinking of a new girl-friend already?'

'No, I am not!' Abruptly he caught hold of her, his hands hurting. 'Do you believe I think of nothing else? Even you must see how impossible it was to find a suitable excuse for not taking Carol Vintis out to dinner. Between you and me she's one very spoiled young woman, and I can't yet afford to pass up an order for two new boats. If only for the sake of the yard and the men, I'm willing to go along with her this once.'

Twisting under his hands, she felt her nerves begin tightening again. Unable to leave well alone, she taunted, 'Really, Macadam, you could be ruining your reputation. Ursula last night, Miss Vintis tonight and me tomorrow—three women in one week! As my grandfather is always saying—what will people think?'

'Nothing to what I'm going to say if you don't be quiet and get out of my sight!' he exclaimed. 'And Zoe,' he spoke more softly, his hands dropping back to his sides after giving her a final shake, 'don't forget to tell Graham you aren't available. Not tomorrow evening,' he added, like an after-thought.

Zoe worked hard for the rest of the day, not putting the cover on her typewriter until after six. Macadam had been down in the yard all afternoon and it bewildered her that she had found herself stealing to the office window several times to watch him. She had to admit he was very attractive, but she couldn't understand why this hadn't impinged itself on her consciousness before. While she had always been aware that he was a good-looking man, she was beginning to notice in detail a lot of little things about him. The way his hair grew thick and dark, inclined to be unruly. The breadth of his shoulders, the proud angle of his head. The way he sometimes used his hands to emphasise a point while he was talking. Was it surprising that women liked him? Zoe thought wretchedly as she shrugged into her coat.

Outside she paused beside him to say goodnight. Most of the men had gone home, but he was still busy, his jacket off, sleeves rolled up, despite the cold. He was lean and tough, his powerful body making her very aware of his undoubted masculinity. He was like the seas, ruthless and free, curiously detached. He might easily sweep a girl off her feet and destroy her, Zoe decided, given half a chance.

Trying not to look at him, she told him she had locked up. He had his own set of keys but needn't bother now to go back to the office unless he wanted to. 'Don't be late for your date,' she said coolly, as she left him.

He had arranged to pick her up at eight-thirty the following evening, and he didn't keep her waiting.

'We ought to be back by midnight,' he assured Janet and Taggart, 'but if it's a little later, don't worry.

'Was your grandfather very upset about Thursday night?' he asked, as they drove away.

'A little,' she smiled ruefully. 'I'd almost forgotten.'

'I lost my temper. I'm sorry.'

'Was that what made you say what you did?'

Macadam was driving through the town. On one side was the sea and promenade, on the other the big hotels and shops and some offices. The promenade was empty at this time of year, but the road was fairly busy. He appeared to be concentrating. 'What did I say?' he murmured absently.

'Never mind,' Zoe replied briefly, leaving him to negotiate the traffic in peace. Of course Macadam didn't want to be reminded of something he had probably said on impulse and now regretted.

She glanced through the car window. The sea looked wild and cold tonight, the sky dark and overcast. It would be dark early, already lights were being switched on in houses and she saw people in front of their windows, drawing their curtains. Soon they arrived at the Findlay residence, and, as they did so, Zoe frowned. She had expected to see the drive lined with cars, but both the drive and the street were empty.

'We must be the first here!' she exclaimed in dismay.

'Strange.' Macadam parked the car and sat for a moment glancing round. 'Well, someone has to be. Come on.'

They got out and she followed him reluctantly to the door. When she would have hung back he put his hand firmly under her arm. He didn't speak as he rang the bell. It echoed eerily inside the house. The whole place seemed deserted. Although she couldn't think why, Zoe shivered.

Macadam rang again, this time impatiently, then the door opened. Ursula Findlay stood before them, clad only in a very transparent négligé. Zoe recognised immediately that nothing quite like it could be purchased in this part of the world. Old Miss Bruce, who stocked the smartest underwear in town, would have fainted clean away at the sight of it.

'Why Reece darling!' Ursula's thickly mascaraed lashes fluttered heavily. 'This is a pleasant surprise.' Then she saw Zoe and her vivid red mouth fell open. 'What's she doing here?'

Reece frowned. 'I understood you were giving a party?'

Ursula was breathing deeply, her shapely breast rose and fell. Zoe wondered how anyone dared wear anything so revealing as a froth of pink lace to answer the door in.

'A party?' Ursula's eyes widened in apparent bewilderment. 'Why, so we are—next week.'

Reece's lips tightened. 'You rang Zoe.'

'Of course.' Ursula managed to look tearfully appealing. 'I was nervous after you were so cross. I would have insisted on speaking to you, if I'd been sure of my reception, but I was clear about the date.'

'You said this evening!' Zoe, almost spluttering with indignation, was unable to keep quiet any longer.

'I told you you ought to get a new secretary, Reece,' Ursula smiled at him sweetly while her négligé slipped lower. 'This girl,' she slung a contemptuous glance at Zoe, 'can't even take a simple message properly.'

'Apparently not.'

Macadam's steely fingers were nearly taking Zoe's elbow apart and she winced with pain. But before she could say anything more in her own defence, Ursula cut in again.

'And I certainly never invited her to any party, this week or any time. I expect she told you I did?'

'Obviously a mistake,' Macadam shrugged, his glance clinging to her half-naked form intently.

'I won't make a fuss.' Ursula almost purred at the

attention she was receiving. Zoe could see her confidence growing as Macadam's eyes ate her up. She felt disgusted with both of them as Ursula continued.

'Why not send Miss Kerr home, Reece darling? Mummy and Daddy are away this weekend and Meg has the night off. There's no one here but me and I'm feeling terribly lonely. I'm sure we can find lots of things to—er—talk about. If you come in while I ring a taxi for Miss Kerr, she can wait for it outside.'

'I'm sorry, Ursula,' Reece sighed, looking for all the world as if he meant it, 'I'm afraid I must take Zoe home myself. I promised her grandfather I would, and you know what he is.'

'I'm afraid I don't.' Ursula's brows rose superciliously. 'But if you must take her home you can always come back.'

'Some other time, perhaps, Ursula,' Macadam replied smoothly, turning Zoe away.

'I can find my own way home!' Zoe cried, feeling inexplicably hurt by the condemnation she thought she read in his eyes.

'No, you can't.'

'How could she! How could you both?' Zoe stammered, as Macadam drew her adamantly back to the car.

'Please be more explicit,' he snapped, reversing savagely out of the drive.

'She was lying, and you believed her!'

'Who said I believed her? But you could have made a mistake.'

'No, I did not!'

'We're all human,' he said curtly. 'Ian had just kissed you, you were still dizzy with delight. You were thinking of him, not your work. If I needed proof of that, the coffee was cold. And one Saturday, to a girl in love, is very much like another.'

'I don't happen to be in love with Ian,' she retorted

heatedly, 'nor was I dizzy with delight or anything else when he kissed me. And I might say,' she added scathingly, 'there's nothing in a kiss to make a girl forget what she's doing.'

'Before you're very much older,' he threatened, 'I might just set out to prove how wrong you are.'

Zoe felt her heart miss a beat, but refused to be sidetracked. 'If you can't see how Ursula must have deliberately planned the whole thing, then nothing I can say is going to convince you. It was obvious she had it all thought out, even down to that ridiculous négligé . . .'

'Actually,' he grinned, 'I thought the négligé was rather fetching.'

'You would!' she retorted scornfully. 'I'd rather be seen dead than wearing anything like it!' Without giving him time to reply, she rushed on, 'Why didn't you tell Miss Findlay that it was you who invited me to her party? You never said a word when she accused me of inviting myself.'

'It seemed a bit pointless to say anything,' he glanced at her impatiently. 'I thought the less said the better— why do you think I hurried you away? I certainly wasn't going to please her by arguing over anything as irrelevant as that.'

'So my feelings don't count?' Zoe said bitterly.

'I'll let you work that out for yourself,' he replied enigmatically. 'Now, before we come to blows, we have to decide how we're going to spend the rest of the evening.'

The rest of the evening? Wasn't he taking her home? 'Would you like to come in and talk to my grandfather?' she suggested.

'No, thank you,' Macadam declined dryly. 'I'm not keen to be read another lecture on how not to compromise his granddaughter. I was thinking of going on somewhere. Have you had dinner?'

'Supper?' She nodded. 'We have dinner in the middle of the day, but when I don't get home for it, when we're busy, Gran makes something more substantial in the evenings. Soup and omelettes, a chop for Grandfather and steamed jam roll with custard, that kind of thing.'

Macadam groaned. 'You're making my mouth water! I've had dinner, but I feel hungry again. Let's find somewhere to eat and have a drink. Somewhere where we can dance for a while as well.'

As Zoe hesitated, for some unknown reason, terribly apprehensive, he took one look at her uncertain face and said softly, 'I suppose I could go back and talk to Ursula, if you really want to go straight home to bed.'

Glancing at him in quick dismay, Zoe swallowed painfully. Why couldn't she bear to think of him doing that? She wasn't absolutely convinced he would, but there was always the possibility. And she refused to spend a restless night wondering.

'I'd love to go anywhere you like,' she smiled, and was startled when she heard him catch his breath and saw the dark look in his eyes.

CHAPTER THREE

As they drove out of town, following the road as it wound inland through numerous glens, Zoe sat back, letting a warm, excited feeling steal over her. It was the first time she had been out like this with Macadam and she was suddenly determined to make the most of it. She would forget Ursula and try and make sure Macadam did as well.

Sometimes, of course, she and Macadam went sailing together. And at sea they were compatible to a degree which never ceased to surprise Zoe whenever she thought of it. When they were out Macadam always took command, but he seldom needed to give an order, because Zoe seemed able to anticipate what he wanted almost before he spoke. He might not say so, but she sensed he enjoyed sailing with her, while for her it had become a kind of secret enchantment. A long day spent crewing for Macadam could tire her but never failed to give intense satisfaction.

On dry land, she realised, they didn't get on nearly so well. In the office and boatyard there was all too often a hint of antagonism between them that could flare readily from a few short words into something little short of a battle. Usually Zoe got the worst of it, for when Macadam really turned on her she was no match for him. If lately he appeared to be humouring her a little, she had no idea why. Maybe it was only her imagination. Certainly during the past few days he had been anything but kind.

'How far are we going?' she asked at last, as the miles sped by.

'Not far now.' He turned his head to glance at her. 'Wait and see.'

Minutes later, he turned into the forecourt of a large hotel. Never having been here before, Zoe didn't recognise it. 'Are they open?' she exclaimed.

'All the year round,' he replied with a quirk. 'There'd be little sense in coming here if they weren't.'

'Ask a silly question,' she muttered, flushing.

'Quite,' he agreed dryly.

It didn't seem a very auspicious beginning. Zoe sighed as she glanced around. There were lots of large cars outside and fur-clad people. 'It looks terribly smart,' she said doubtfully.

'So do you.' Macadam's mouth tightened, then relaxed in a wry grin, 'I'm sure you won't disgrace me.'

Her soft mouth drooping, she sighed glumly, 'I hope not.'

'Oh, for God's sake!' he snapped, 'don't tell me you've suddenly developed an inferiority complex? I might suffer your sharp little tongue, but never that.'

'I'm sure you'd manage,' she retorted bitterly, 'You usually give as good as I send.'

'I hope not,' he said flintily. 'Sometimes I feel quite battered.'

'Very funny!' she replied, without humour, wondering if he had any idea the effect he had on her. Sometimes, when he let rip, she was certain she couldn't have felt worse if he had physically assaulted her. She shivered, her hand reaching out in a sudden blind panic for the door.

'Here, let me help.'

As she fumbled, Macadam glanced at her anxiously and leant over to release the door catch. 'Don't forget your seat-belt,' he said, as she made to get out.

'My . . .? Oh, yes, of course.' She tried to laugh at

her own stupidity, but her laughter seemed strangled in her throat.

With a sigh, Macadam dealt with the belt, too, hooking it up above her head, an operation which, of necessity, brought him very close. 'What's wrong, Zoe?' he asked as she flinched. 'I'm not going to bite.' His fingers curved her small, rounded chin, turning her face towards him.

'It was nothing.' She kept her lashes lowered, unable to look at him, the feelings which swept over her no more understandable than they had been before. She was aware of a potent, almost tangible attraction, something as yet nameless between them which made her terribly apprehensive. Her thoughts fluttered wildly. Mentally she saw a keg of dynamite and a box of matches. If someone wasn't careful the whole thing could blow up.

Suddenly Macadam lowered his head and kissed her quite gently on the mouth. Taking her face between his hands, he tipped it backwards, his fingers winding through her tumbled hair. His lips touched hers lightly and she could feel her heartbeats racing. The kiss deepened and they were pressing together, oblivious of place and time.

Then abruptly she was free and he was saying tersely, 'Go on, Zoe, get out.'

Panic rising in her, Zoe turned to obey, then as suddenly paused, catching a glimpse of his expression. Something glittered in his eyes, she didn't know what, but it made her tremble. 'Why did you kiss me like that?' she whispered.

For a moment Macadam didn't reply, a faint red touching his hard cheeks. When he loooked at her again his face was quite blank. 'Perhaps I thought it would make a change from our continual bickering?'

She continued to stare at him with puzzled, doubtful eyes, which still held something of the unawakened candour of a child. 'If you say so,' she muttered, feeling strangely dissatisfied.

Impatiently, his eyes hardening, he sighed, 'You don't have to look like that, Zoe—as though you're investigating a crime. These things happen between a man and woman; they're rarely planned—or explainable.'

There was no logical way she could deny that, and while she might be flattered that he had referred to her as a woman, it didn't help that, at the moment, she felt more like a lost child. Emotions she neither recognised or knew how to deal with were rushing through her, and she sensed, with a surge of humiliation, that Macadam was aware of her inexperience as much as she was herself.

'Let's go in, Zoe,' he said curtly, his eyes lingering repressively on her pale face. 'I don't feel like sitting here all night.'

The hotel was surprisingly busy. The dining-room was just closing, but they were serving a variety of light suppers in the bar. Macadam ordered scampi and chips and a bottle of wine. Zoe was surprised to find how hungry she was and enjoyed the meal very much, something she hadn't expected to do, not after what had just taken place.

Macadam didn't talk much. He looked rather tired, she thought. He had probably been out half the previous night with Carol Vintis. A sharp needle of jealousy pierced Zoe as she stared at his dark, attractive face. What had they talked about until the early hours, she wondered bleakly—or, more to the point, what had they done?

Her cheeks coloured when he glanced up to catch her gazing at him. 'Now what?' he asked sardonically.

'Nothing . . .' she stammered, finding his straight glance unnerving. 'Well,' again she hesitated, 'I was just thinking how tired you look.'

'So I have to prove I'm not,' he said lazily, 'or you'll go on believing I didn't get Miss Vintis home until dawn.'

She flushed guiltily, unable to deviate. 'How did you guess?'

'It wasn't difficult to put two and two together,' he said dryly. 'I can assure you Miss Vintis arrived home at a very respectable hour. Too respectable for her liking, I suspect.'

'Then it can only be Ursula?' she frowned.

'Zoe!' he exclaimed, his eyes glinting. 'You're like a dog with a bone!'

Bitterly she returned his impatient glance. 'I'm only concerned for you, for the good of the yard, if you like.' Even to her own ears that sounded very trite and she looked away from him angrily.

'I appreciate your concern,' Macadam said soberly.

For all his straight face, she felt instinctively that he was laughing at her. 'You have so many women!' she exaggerated outrageously.

'But I never think of more than one at once,' he assured her, 'and I'm here with you, tonight.'

As Zoe flushed, as if to punish her, he placed a mocking hand over hers as it lay on the table. Embarrassed, she snatched it away. 'I'm not one of your women!' she hissed.

'Wouldn't you like to be?' he wondered idly.

'I was never good at competing,' she retorted mutinously.

'If the competition involved sharp answers you would win hands down,' he said grimly. 'Don't worry,' he smiled without humour as she shrank from him, 'I'm not going to slap you—or kiss you again. You don't imagine I would wish to repeat that experience with such a prickly little hedgehog?'

'Hedgehog?' Remembering how she had almost melted in his arms, Zoe felt mortally wounded.

'Yes,' he insisted firmly. 'You curl up inside yourself whenever I attempt to touch you.'

'Self-defence,' she managed to murmur.

'I didn't notice any barriers going up when Graham kissed you?' Macadam returned cynically, 'nor when Freddy Vintis smiled at you.'

'That was—I mean, they are different,' she said carefully, having no idea where the difference lay. In her heart she knew she considered Macadam superior to every other man she knew, but he must never suspect that.

She was startled but relieved when he rose to his feet abruptly, pulling her to hers and dragging her towards the bar, as if suddenly tired of such pointless conversation. He ordered something from the barman, who set fresh drinks before them. Zoe almost grabbed hers, thinking it would give her fresh courage. Drinking recklessly, she spluttered and choked. It was lemonade and she had drunk it too fast. The bubbles went up her nose and she sneezed.

'Oh, I do hate you!' she gasped as Macadam threw back his head and laughed. He did spare her the ignominy of thumping her on the back, but she was too cross to feel grateful.

'You swallowed that as though you needed it,' he chuckled, passing his handkerchief. 'You should have seen your face when you discovered it was just lemonade!'

Before she could reply a voice hailed them. It was the Vintis family, at least the father, daughter and son. Carol Vintis signalled wildly as she approached, as if terrified they might run away. 'Reece, Mr Macadam!' she cried. 'This is a pleasant surprise!'

'For some people!' Zoe muttered, as was frequently her habit, under her breath. Taking heed of Macadam's cooling glance, she changed her scowl to a smile.

He greeted the Vintises politely. 'Zoe and I are going next door to dance,' he told them.

'We've just finished dinner,' Freddy drawled, staring at Zoe admiringly. 'It's not a bad little place. Carol said——' he turned to Macadam, 'you recommended it to her last night.'

'Yes,' Carol interrupted eagerly, 'that's why we decided to try it out. My mother wouldn't come as she and Dad had a quarrel and aren't speaking to each other, but I'm sure she'll be sorry she's missed it.'

Charles Vintis said nothing and Zoe glanced at him curiously. Macadam said nothing either, his face giving, as usual, no indication of what he was thinking.

'Did you say you were going to dance, Reece?' Carol asked, smiling at him while ignoring Zoe. 'Would you mind if we joined you?'

Tell her no, Zoe prayed silently, resenting such an intrusion. The evening had already been marred by one or two incidents but this seemed the worst of the lot.

Macadam, of course, said no such thing. 'We won't be staying long but you're welcome to join us if you like.'

'Did you arrange to meet them here?' Zoe muttered as she circled the spacious floor of the room adjoining the bar in Macadam's arms.

'No,' he replied tersely.

'It looks very suspicious!'

'For heaven's sake, Zoe, don't turn this evening into a greater fiasco than it already is.' His arms tightened almost cruelly.

Zoe gasped. She had never been out with him like this before; never been so near him, apart from the odd, mistaken incident she didn't care to remember. As they danced, as when they sailed, they seemed to fit perfectly together, but her body was unbearably sensitive. As Macadam's hand moved restlessly on her slender back, his fingers were leaving a blaze of fire wherever they touched. She tried to look cool, to be cool, but the sensation he was generating inside her threatened to burn her up.

'Macadam?' she whispered, emotion clouding her beautiful almond-shaped eyes. 'I feel . . .'

'Never mind how you feel!' He roughly pushed a little distance between them, breaking the crushing embrace he was imposing on her.

Even as he pushed her away, she wanted to cling to him. She continued to stare up at him, her skin prickling, her eyes dazed. When she realised his face was a cold mask, she felt her whole body tighten rigidly and forced herself to look away.

Humiliation brought a quick colour to her cheeks. Her voice husky, she exclaimed, 'Sometimes I don't understand you!'

'You certainly don't understand yourself,' he spoke between his teeth. 'Until you know what you're doing I'd advise you not to play with fire—unless you're prepared to accept more than you bargained for.'

Stirring uneasily, Zoe's lashes flickered upwards. So he was warning her not to interfere between him and any of his women again. Bitterly she said, 'I get the message . . .'

'I doubt if you have.' He watched her enigmatically, but he seemed a little more relaxed.

'I wish I'd gone out with Ian,' she muttered. 'At least he's easy to understand.'

'Of course he is!' Macadam bit back. 'No complications there, just one thought in his head—how to get the girl into bed as quickly as possible. If she happens to be a naïve little virgin, all the better. Graham loves new experiences, especially sexual ones. He wouldn't believe some situations call for delicate handling. A man's passion might sometimes threaten to get the better of him, but he could scarcely call himself a man if he wasn't capable of a little patient restraint. Graham doesn't know the meaning of the word. He would enjoy himself all right, but would you?'

Zoe stared at him, almost too shocked to speak. 'Ian's not like that!'

Pityingly he shook his head. 'Want to bet? No,' he added sharply, 'you might just be foolish enough to try and prove me wrong. Just let my words penetrate the childish crush you have on him, Zoe. Don't throw away your most precious possession on a man who doesn't deserve it.'

Incensed, she retorted. 'Better that, perhaps, than saving yourself for a man who doesn't want you!'

Macadam's eyes glinted. 'And who, do you imagine, doesn't want you?'

Delicate colour rushed to her face. 'I—I was just talking generally.'

'Well, I'm not.'

She met his eyes resentfully. 'I don't think you have any right to talk to me like this. You've been insulting.'

'I'd like to do more than insult you!'

Aware of his mounting anger, she wasn't surprised at his obvious relief when the dance finished. Yet she was even more conscious of her own disappointment. In spite of the harsh words they had exchanged she felt oddly cheated. She had been looking forward so much to dancing with Macadam, but all he had done was lecture her. Bitterly she mocked herself for having expected anything else.

Charles Vintis was sitting at their table drinking steadily, his eyes fixed on a voluptuous, lone blonde. Zoe wondered what his wife was like, what they had quarrelled about.

Macadam, after an impatient glance in Zoe's direction, asked Carol to dance. As they took to the floor, Zoe heard Carol laugh, 'Daddy's got his eye on another woman, I'm afraid.'

So that was the trouble, Zoe thought. Charles

Vintis's face was still good-looking but rather weak.
As Freddy Vintis swept her away without so much as
asking, she was too curious about his father to object.

'Is your father unhappy?' she asked, then immediately felt terribly embarrassed. 'I'm sorry,' she
apologised, 'I shouldn't have said anything, it's none
of my business.'

Freddy merely laughed. 'Think nothing of it, honey.
The old man's affairs aren't exactly a secret, but then
his wife's frigid. She's his third wife, of course, no
relation of mine. Carol and I get on all right with her,
but we understand the old man, too. He has to get his
kicks somewhere. The wonder is they're still together.'

Zoe hesitated uncertainly, not sure how to reply. If
she was shocked it was as much with Freddy as his
father. To her it seemed incomprehensible how anyone
could speak so frankly and crudely about their parents
to a stranger. If she couldn't admire the way in which
Charles Vintis apparently lived his life, she found she
couldn't admire Freddy much, either.

'Do you want to hear more?'

Startled, she shook her head, then saw from his
glance that he thought her old-fashioned and it amused
him. Sharply she said. 'I do know what goes on, but I
don't particularly wish to discuss it. Besides, not
everyone's the same.'

'People in these parts, I suppose, never leave the
straight and narrow.'

'Oh, don't be so silly!' she sighed, feeling suddenly
irritated.

'No,' he laughed. 'Take your Mr Macadam, for instance. I bet he's no angel!'

'I'd rather not talk about him,' Zoe said stiffly.

'Then just look,' Freddy whispered. 'Just look at
him, honey.'

Involuntarily, as if Freddy's racy way of talking
drove her on, Zoe obeyed. Turning her head, she was

stunned to see Carol Vintis dancing with Macadam, her arms wrapped tightly around his neck, her head nestling against his shoulder. As Zoe gazed, Macadam bent to whisper something, and she could have sworn his lips touched Carol's cheek.

'He's all man, that one, isn't he?' Freddy grinned. 'Trust Carol to find him straight away!'

Macadam raised his head. Across the space of a few feet, his glance met Zoe's and she dragged her eyes from the open mockery in his. How could he? she wondered bitterly. And how could she defend him when he was so clearly everything Freddy made him out to be!

When Freddy, suddenly losing interest in his family and Macadam, murmured softly, 'I'm looking for a little sexy diversion myself, honey. How about having dinner with me next week?' she was tempted to agree.

Fortunately, in time, she came to her senses and refused. 'I'm not sure what I'll be doing. If you like you can give me a ring.'

She hoped he would forget, or meet someone else before he remembered to. She sensed Freddy's main trouble was boredom and almost suggested he'd be wiser looking for a job, rather than a girl-friend.

A little later she and Macadam left.

'Did you enjoy yourself?' he enquired, after a rather silent journey home.

'As much as I expected to, I suppose,' she replied coldly.

'Now where have I gone wrong?' he muttered dryly. 'You show a remarkable lack of enthusiasm.'

That stung her. 'You surely couldn't expect me to be enthusiastic, not after the way you've been behaving? Twice, this evening . . .'

'Wait a minute!' he threw up a furious hand. 'Twice? That sounds interesting, darling. Let's discuss the first time, shall we, and take it from there? You're suggesting I've been making a fool of myself?'

Glancing at him quickly, she saw his eyes were glinting with anger, and knew she had overstepped the mark. Well, for once she didn't care. How dared he call her darling, with that look in his eyes, and sarcasm dripping off the edge of his tongue? 'I might be,' she spluttered defiantly, getting herself all mixed up. 'The first time was when you looked at Ursula in that terrible négligé, as if you'd like to have eaten her up.'

That was gross exaggeration, of course, but in situations like this it wasn't easy to find exactly the right words. As she drew a shallow breath, Macadam prompted tightly, 'And the next?'

Zoe whispered, before her courage failed her, 'The way you were dancing with Carol Vintis. She had her arms around your neck.'

'Yes,' he said softly, as though the memory of it was pleasant and already dispersing some of his anger, 'she had. And what do you suggest I should have done about it? You didn't like it? Is that what all this fuss is about?'

'It looked extremely silly!' she answered stiffly.

'Anything like that often does to other people,' he shot her a coolly mocking glance. 'Haven't you tried it yourself?'

'No!'

'Well, you ought to,' he advised. 'I think you'd enjoy it.'

'What makes you think so?' she asked tautly.

'I kissed you, remember.' His eyes slipped over her fraught young face. 'I'd say you have definite potential.'

The hint of amusement in his voice hurt, inciting her to retort coolly, 'Freddy Vintis seems to think so, too.'

The change in Macadam was imperceptible, but she sensed it. She wasn't surprised when he asked, 'Does that mean he wants you to go out with him?'

'Yes.'

'And you refused, of course? I did warn you.'

'I told him to give me a ring next week.'

'And when he does, you can tell him you're otherwise engaged.'

Defiantly, Zoe stared at him, her hands clenched. 'And if I'm not?'

'Then I'll make sure you are,' he snapped curtly. 'Even if I have to take you out again myself.'

She could have hit him for that, with something primitive moving inside her; in fact she almost did. While she hadn't liked the way he had neglected her, this evening, for Carol Vintis, this seemed by far the greater insult. 'I wouldn't dream of putting you to so much trouble!' she cried sharply, as they reached her home.

'Oh, it wouldn't be all that much trouble,' he drawled, a hint of self-derision in his eyes.

'Goodnight, Macadam!' she said coldly, jumping out of the car before he could help her and disappearing into the house.

Her grandparents were in bed, Zoe was relieved. In her bedroom she threw off the long dress she had bought only that afternoon, letting it fall in a silken heap on the floor. She was glad she hadn't allowed Macadam to pay for it, but she wished she could forget how she had felt when he had held her close and his hands had roamed over it restlessly. Impatiently she picked it up, thrusting it carelessly into the back of her wardrobe. She didn't think she would ever want to wear it again, but if it was out of sight it might be easier to forget things she would rather not remember.

Sunday, which usually passed too quickly, dragged. After lunch, despite her intention not to, she went to the boatyard where she often found Macadam at weekends. When he went sailing he frequently took her, not by prior arrangement, but because they both took it for granted that she would go. Today, however, he was nowhere to be seen, and trying to ignore her deep disappointment, Zoe turned away.

Disconsolately, she wandered back through the town. The weather was cold but bright, the choppy seas would have presented the kind of challenge she and Macadam loved. Across the Firth of Lorn she could see the mountains of Mull and thought nostalgically of the miles of untamed ocean. She had other friends whom she could have gone sailing with, but at that moment she could think of no one but Macadam.

When she reached the office, next morning, the telephone was ringing stridently. As she picked it up, panting out the number, Macadam's voice rasped in her ear. 'Where the hell have you been?'

It was barely eight, but she didn't waste time reminding him. Instead she asked quickly, 'Where are you?'

'I'm in bed,' he snapped, as if she was a fool to have asked. 'Where do you think I'd be?'

She'd begun unbuttoning her coat after her rush upstairs to answer the phone. Now her fingers froze. 'In bed?' She heard her voice rising in panic and controlled it. 'What are you doing in bed, Macadam? Have you had an accident?'

'I couldn't have been worse if I had,' he croaked. 'I've got a cold.'

'A—cold?' She knew she must sound faintly incredulous, but she couldn't help it. She couldn't remember Macadam ever having a cold, or even a day's illness in his life. 'I—I'm sorry,' she stammered as the lengthening silence seemed to call for some expression of sympathy. 'You'll be late, then ... What time can we expect you?'

'Don't be so damned stupid!' he exclaimed

furiously. 'Do you think I'd be lying here if I were capable of getting up?'

'You—you actually are in bed?'

His sigh was quite audible. 'I've already told you twice!'

'I'm sorry . . .' Her stunned mind began slowly to work again. 'Have you called the doctor?'

'No I have not.' He cleared his throat hoarsely. 'He couldn't do anything for me, these things only take time.'

Zoe swallowed hard. 'But if you're really ill . . .'

Impatiently he cut in, 'Stop making stupid remarks, Zoe, and get up here at once. I'll expect you in not more than ten minutes. Take the pick-up.'

'Hadn't I better wait until the mail comes in?'

'You can bring that later. Just do as I ask.'

For a few seconds Zoe's thoughts were in chaos, as she tried to pull herself together. She was so used to Macadam standing over her, telling her what to do, keeping an eagle eye on her; without him she felt lost.

'Whatever can be wrong with him?' she found herself wondering aloud.

'Who are you talking to?' Ian asked.

Quickly she spun around. Ian was lounging against the door watching her, his hands lazily in his pockets. 'Myself,' she snapped, refusing to be embarrassed.

'Where's the boss?' he eyed her white face curiously, 'Is something up?'

'He's ill!' she gasped, feeling suddenly, terribly anxious. 'Don't ask me how ill—he may be dying!'

Ian's brows quirked derisively. 'Dying people aren't usually able to shout down the phone.'

'Perhaps not,' she admitted reluctantly, biting her lip, 'but he did sound a bit peculiar—not quite himself.'

'Ha! That would be funny,' Ian laughed soberly. 'Well, let's make the most of it. The jailor's away so

the bird can play.' He swept her into his arms and
kissed her. Glancing over his shoulder, he murmured
with assumed astonishment, 'What, no Macadam?'

Angrily, Zoe pushed him away. 'Much as you dislike
being reminded of the fact, Ian, he does pay us good
salaries—and I wish you wouldn't make a habit of
kissing me during office hours.'

'Fat lot of chance I get out of them!' he grumbled.

Recalling Macadam's warning, she glanced at Ian
suspiciously as she gathered up some pads and things
she thought she might need. 'If anyone rings tell them
I shouldn't be long, if it's something you can't see to
yourself.'

'You mean you're actually going up there to see
him?'

'Boss's orders,' she replied.

She had never been to Macadam's house before, but
she knew exactly where to find it. It had belonged to
his uncle and lay in the hills to the south of the town.
Zoe loved it on sight. True, it looked old and grey and
rather shabby, but it fitted so beautifully into the
landscape that she couldn't help feeling it might have
grown there. Behind it was a protective half-circle of
rocky hills and tall trees, while below, at the edge of
the grounds, the pounding sea filled the narrow chan-
nel between the mainland and the island of Kerrera. A
few hardy souls were out sailing, but for once she
didn't gaze at them with envy. She was too anxious
about Macadam this morning to spare the time to do
that.

She rang the bell and waited, then rang again when
no one answered. Eventually Macadam himself opened
the door. Zoe stared at him, frowning. He was wearing
an old towelling robe, almost too short to be decent,
and a faint colour stole to her cheeks.

He appeared to be annoyed. 'If I had any sense I'd
give you a month's notice,' he snapped.

'A month's notice?' Her face went pale again. 'But why?'

'Because I don't care to employ a girl with no brains,' he replied sharply. 'What the hell do you mean, standing here ringing the bell, dragging me from my bed when I'm ill?'

With a few words he could make her feel very young and gauche, and she resented it. She had raced to him at a breakneck speed and apparently this was all the thanks she was going to get. 'I'm sorry,' she said stiffly, 'I didn't mean to fetch you downstairs. I thought your woman might be here.'

'Here we go again!' he glared. 'What woman, now, am I being accused of harbouring?'

'Your daily help. She's the one I'm talking about,' Zoe glared back at him.

'I don't have one, just someone who cleans up once a week. I thought you knew.'

'No, I didn't. How could I? You never tell me anything.'

'I thought a good secretary knew everything,' he jibed, 'without having to be told.'

'I may not know everything,' she retorted sharply, 'but I do know that if you're ill you shouldn't be standing out here.'

'Point taken.' He turned, leading the way upstairs, obviously expecting her to follow.

Closing the outer door quickly behind her, she chased after him, trying to keep her eyes off the flexing muscles in his long, powerful legs as he took the stairs two at a time. He didn't seem all that ill.

The house was large. Inside, from what she could see of it, she would have described it as shabby but comfortable. Following Macadam into his bedroom, she glanced around curiously. Like the rest of the house, it was spacious but neglected.

She heard him mutter derisively, from where he sat

on the edge of his bed, 'I'm the one in need of attention, not the decor.'

'Sorry,' she didn't think he could be serious, 'I was
just looking.'

'So—what's wrong with looking at me?'

Her eyes returned to him reluctantly, a pulse beginning to beat rapidly at the base of her throat. 'I—
I'm not used to seeing men with so little on.'

'Well, enjoy yourself while you can,' he muttered
jeeringly, at the hot colour in her face. 'Plenty of
women in this town would give a lot to be in your
shoes.'

Zoe stared at him angrily, but refused to be taunted
into an argument. 'I'm sure you didn't ask me to come
all the way here just to tell me that,' she said coldly.

'I'm ill,' he excused himself, 'although you don't
seem to believe it. You haven't even asked how I am.'

CHAPTER FOUR

ZOE would never have believed that Macadam, always so arrogant, self-sufficient and hard, could feel so sorry for himself. Or was it just self-pity? Now that she was able to take a longer, closer look at him, he really did look ill. He hadn't had a shave since Saturday, she felt certain, and beneath the dark growth of beard his face seemed very white. His hair was uncombed and his eyes red-rimmed, as she had sometimes seen them after a long, rough day at sea.

'Is it just a cold, or something else?' she asked carefully.

'I've probably picked up this 'flu bug that's going,' he said briefly. 'My legs feel next to useless and I'm aching all over.'

Zoe stared at him anxiously, suddenly almost trembling. Because she didn't understand why she should be so concerned, she suggested quickly, 'Would you like me to go home and fetch my grandmother? If you won't have the doctor, she's very good.'

'No, thank you,' he replied dryly. 'With all due respect to your grandmother, Taggart would feel obliged to come along to chaperon her, and that would just about finish me off!'

Well, if he could still joke . . . Zoe sighed. 'I think you'd better get back into bed anyway.'

'Yes,' he agreed meekly, and began peeling off his dressing-gown.

She turned her head quickly, fixing her eyes on the window. She didn't think he had anything on underneath and felt at once both outraged and excited. Her rage she could understand but not the excitement. It threatened to overwhelm her completely, drawing her towards Macadam when she only wanted to flee from him.

'For God's sake, Zoe!' she heard him snap, 'I'm not about to assault you, I'm a sick man.'

How sick? Feeling herself quiver, she remained silent.

'You can look now,' he mocked.

He was in bed, the blankets piled up to his chin. He looked far from comfortable and she wished she had offered to make his bed before he got into it again. Uncertainly, she smiled at him, 'Can I get you anything?'

'I thought you'd never ask,' he muttered. 'A cup of tea would be nice. Maybe a boiled egg and some toast as well. Better make it two slices and some marmalade.'

'All that . . .?' she gasped.

'I can't promise I'll have the strength to eat it,' Macadam said grimly.

'You'd better tell me where the kitchen is.'

'Of course,' and he proceeded to give her the necessary instructions.

The kitchen was pleasant, but every surface was littered. While the kettle boiled and the eggs cooked Zoe did a quick whip round and tidied up. What Macadam needed was someone to look after him and the obvious answer was a wife. Suddenly, Zoe felt guilty. She was always pleased when his affairs were over, but perhaps it would be better if he married one of the women he took out? Yet the thought of Macadam married was strangely repugnant to her. She liked him as he was, bad temper and everything. A wife might change him too much, she told herself.

If she was aware of other reasons why she didn't want Macadam married, she wasn't ready to face them yet. She decided to concentrate on getting him well again; the boatyard never seemed the same without him.

After setting a tray neatly, she added a rack of toast and took it up to his room. He was still in bed, his eyes closed.

'I'm back,' she announced loudly. 'Are you asleep?'

Wincing, he opened his eyes. 'How could I be, with the noise you're making?'

'I've brought you your breakfast,' she said severely, 'but if you don't behave I'll take it away again.'

'Oh, no!' He sat up, in sharp protest, and the blankets dropped down to his waist. 'This smells almost as good as you look.'

'No need to try and butter me up.' Zoe placed the tray with a small thump before him, managing to ignore the surge of pleasure which went through her. 'You can't be that bad!'

'Because my appetite and appreciation of a pretty woman is still undiminished?' he taunted.

She poured him a cup of tea without replying, doing her best to keep her eyes off his broad, hair-roughened chest. She had seen him stripped to the waist in the yard and at sea often enough, but here, in the intimacy of his bedroom, she was conscious of him as she had never been before, on those other occasions.

'I prefer my tea in the cup, rather than the saucer,' he pointed out, as her hand trembled.

She almost poured it over his head. Instead, maintaining her dignity, she passed it to him in continuing silence.

'I've been thinking,' said Macadam, tipping half the contents of the sugar basin in his cup and stirring contemplatively, 'and I've come to the conclusion that what I need here is a housekeeper.'

'You mean—a wife?'

'It might come to that,' he glanced at her bent head

quickly. 'Do you think I'd get many candidates for the post?'

As though he couldn't guess! Zoe busied herself putting the tea-cosy she had found over the teapot to keep it warm. 'You wouldn't be very easy to live with,' she said at last, feeling quite shaken.

'But some girl might be willing to put up with me?' he teased gently. 'How about you?'

'Oh, don't be silly,' she snapped, hurt and angry that he should be mocking her in this way. Heaven help her if he ever guessed she was beginning to think of him a little too much for her own good! Better that he should believe she was half in love with somebody else.

Apprehension drove her to add impulsively, 'I think I'd prefer someone like Ian.'

'Graham?' Macadam's voice was suddenly harsh. 'What's he been up to?'

'Nothing,' she stammered, her cheeks bright red.

'He's been kissing you again?' Macadam's eyes smouldered. 'This morning, I presume?'

'He was just fooling.' Zoe was bitterly regretting saying anything. 'You know what he is.'

'I know what he is,' Macadam snapped contemptuously, 'and it's enlightening that you prefer him to me. Perhaps when I get out of here I should take a leaf out of his book—Early morning kisses in the office, rendezvous, no doubt, in the depths of the night. What does Taggart think of Graham seducing you in the dark on the sea-front? It must be time I had a word with your grandfather about him. Taggart's so busy watching out for my probable immorality that he's missing what's going on under his very nose. You'd better be prepared to be dragged to the altar, after he's heard what I have to say!'

'Macadam, please!' Zoe felt near to tears. 'None of that's true, you've got it all wrong—and you're making yourself ill!'

'I am ill,' he fell back against his pillows with a groan, 'and you're making me worse.'

'I'm not wasting your time at the office,' she protested wildly. 'I wouldn't dream of doing such a thing. Why, I was only saying to Ian, before I left, how well you pay us.'

'Why did he need reminding?' Macadam asked flintily.

Zoe gazed at him, her face hot with angry frustration. Even when ill, Macadam never missed a thing!

While she searched for a reply which wouldn't involve Ian any further, he pushed his barely touched tray towards her. 'Here, take this, my appetite's gone. You'd better get out of here before my temperature soars any higher. I've made out a list of things I'd like done, you can give it to Donald or one of the foremen. Oh, and yes, when the mail comes in bring it to me immediately.'

Zoe was almost glad to go, although she had a guilty feeling she hadn't done nearly enough. She hoped Macadam would be in a better mood when she came back. His insinuations regarding Ian and herself had annoyed and frightened her, but she decided not to take them too seriously. She was sure he wouldn't have said what he had done if he'd been well. He had probably had a bad night and begun imagining things. His allegations about her grandfather seemed to prove it. She found it impossible to believe that her grandfather suspected Macadam had designs on her, especially when he knew Macadam was even stricter with her than he was. He might have kissed her, but he hadn't meant her to take it seriously. It had probably been his way of teasing her a little, of letting her know he considered she was growing up.

When she returned, later in the morning, he had been up and shaved. He had gone back to bed but, she fancied for her sake, was wearing a pair of thin silk pyjamas. The house was lovely and warm, so he must have turned the central heating on. When he asked, with a slight smile, if she approved, Zoe replied with a hint of impatience. 'If you'd told me about it when I was here before I could have switched it on myself, and I needn't have worried all the way to the office about you being cold. I didn't notice the radiators and even got Jim Weir to chop me some sticks so I could light you a fire.'

Macadam didn't appear at all repentant. If anything his eyes glinted with something more like satisfaction as they rested on her indignant face. 'My uncle had central heating installed years ago, then found he preferred being on the cold side. I'm afraid I often forget about it. I have an immersion heater and usually use that for baths.'

He seemed as determined as she was to forget their earlier dissension, and for a while the atmosphere was as calm as a summer's day.

'I brought the portable,' Zoe told him, after they had gone briefly through the letters she had considered urgent. 'I'll go and see to these in the kitchen while you rest.'

'Find the study,' he grunted. 'You'll be more comfortable there.'

'I have some bones for soup. In fact it's already on,' she confessed. 'I'd rather work in the kitchen as it will be easier to look after it. We could have lunch at one. By then I should have most of the correspondence ready for you to sign.'

To her surprise Macadam made no further protest, and her heart ached suddenly as she saw he looked quite exhausted. On impulse she crossed over to the bed and began tidying it, smoothing the sheets and straightening his pillows.

As she leaned over him, absorbed in what she was doing, her thick, glossy hair fell over her face and she tossed it back impatiently.

She heard his brief laughter, low and throaty. 'You ought to get yourself a ribbon, but it smells good.'

His compliment, if it was meant as one, made her recall how she had felt when he had kissed her and brought a surge of delicate colour to her cheeks. In a rush the emotion she had experienced then welled through her vividly. Again she found herself struggling with her breath and felt her knees weaken.

He glanced up at her with heavy-lidded eyes, a touch of fever and something else in their depth. 'No kiss for me, I see?' he remarked dryly.

Her breath inhaled audibly as she jerked upright. 'You're either joking or delirious,' she snapped.

'I wasn't delirious on Saturday.'

'No,' she retorted contemptuously, 'there was no excuse for you then.'

'I don't recall having to use much force,' he mocked softly, 'nor do I remember any great struggle.' Persuasively, with a taunting smile, he caught hold of her hand, 'Perhaps we should repeat the experiment and see?'

'You're despicable!' she gasped, staring at him, her green eyes wide with alarm. Her heart beating wildly, she wondered what she would do if he dragged her down to him. She had never been in bed with a man before, and, as her eyes fell on Macadam's long, powerful body, she was suddenly able only to feel, not think. Stunned, her glance wandered over his dark, inscrutable face. Why had she never noticed what a sensuous mouth he had? Previously she had merely seen the way it straightened tightly when he was annoyed. Now she noticed the bottom lip was quite full, the top one thinner but curved. It revealed a man of fairly strong passions, who might one day be at the mercy of them. She shuddered to think of the girl he might be with if that happened, and for no reason she could think of she felt her lips part warmly under his, although he was doing nothing more than grasp her hand.

As though he no longer cared for the touch of her, he flung her hand away. 'It's funny,' he sneered, 'very funny indeed, how you defend Graham's right to kiss you like a virago yet denounce any similar aspirations on my part in no uncertain fashion. God knows I have no wish to kiss you again, but it has proved, if nothing else, to be an interesting exercise.'

His curt, crisp words effectively brought Zoe to her senses. Had he put his arms round her, she realised, she might not have been able to resist him. As it was, the open scorn on his face made her fully aware of what she was inviting.

'I was only trying to tidy your bed,' she choked, 'not get into it!'

'How kind,' he replied nastily. 'Remind me to pay you a little extra this week, for all the trouble you've gone to.'

She could cheerfully have hit him, as she had been tempted to on several occasions lately, but his derisiveness did revive her slipping composure. 'Sometimes I hate you, Macadam!' she cried, almost running from the room.

When the letters were finished, in a neatly typed pile, she placed them on a tray along with two mugs of hot soup and a plate of warm, crusty bread. She then made coffee and put it in a large flask to keep hot. Glancing around the pleasant kitchen, she felt like having her lunch down here, in peace, but somehow the thought of Macadam in his huge, lonely bedroom made her decide to risk his jibes and temper and keep him company.

He enjoyed the soup but could only manage one small piece of bread. He had two cups of coffee, though, and she thought he looked a little better. He signed the letters, then lay gazing at her drowsily. Judging him to be almost asleep, Zoe prepared to leave, and was startled when he spoke to her.

'You'll have to look in at tea-time. I'll probably have something else for you to do.'

Zoe nodded. She had been going to, anyway, but he needn't know that now.

'Meanwhile,' he went on, as if he didn't intend she should go back to the office to twiddle her thumbs, 'don't forget to ring Pentlands and see what's happened to that order we sent in, and you'd better tell Ian to get over to Dalmally and see old Major Campbell about that boat of his. He's neglected it so long it's beyond repair, I'm afraid. It's nothing but a bucket of rust.'

'Couldn't he ring the Major up?' Zoe asked. 'It's a long way to Dalmally.'

'It will keep him out of mischief,' said Macadam enigmatically. 'And if he isn't pleased about it, you can soften the blow by mentioning that I want him to go to Mexico on Thursday instead of me. I won't be fit enough.'

'Not fit enough?' she repeated in astonishment.

'Don't stare at me like that!' he snapped. 'I may not look at death's door, but I feel pretty rotten and I know when I'm beaten.'

'It would be the first time! Zoe blinked disbelievingly, as relieved as she was surprised that Macadam was prepared to be sensible at last. He had the 'flu and although, as he said, he might not look too bad, it was very weakening. It was a good thing he had realised in time. In the past he had always ignored the least sign of weakness in himself. If ever she had, on rare occasions, questioned his fitness to travel, he had dismissed her anxiety brusquely and gone ahead with his plans.

'It's rather important, though, isn't it, this trip?' she asked doubtfully. 'Do you think Ian can manage?'

'I'd like to know why not,' he said coldly. 'Hasn't he more letters after his name than I have, and a tongue,' he added, with a sour glance, 'which impresses most people. We had no complaints when he went to France last year, and the French are among the best yachtsmen in the world.'

'I still believe,' she began, 'that it might be wiser to wait until you can go yourself. After all, Mexico isn't France . . .'

'Don't worry,' he cut in, obviously believing she was concerned for Ian's safety, 'he won't come to any harm and he should scarcely be gone a week.'

When she broke the news to Ian he was jubilant. 'Say that again!' His face broke into incredulous smiles. After she did he was still incredulous. 'To be perfectly honest, I never thought he'd ever give me a chance like this. You're sure whatever he's got hasn't affected his head?'

Zoe refused to be amused. 'He seems to have faith in you.' She looked at Ian sternly. 'Just make sure you justify it and don't do anything between now and Thursday to make him change his mind.'

Ian didn't. He worked hard on the new design and, as if he sensed Macadam's continuing approbation might in some way be bound up with his attitude towards Zoe, he made no attempt to kiss her again. He only asked if she would have dinner with him when he came back. 'If the trip is successful, that is,' he added wryly.

'Well, if it is, we'll certainly have something to celebrate,' Zoe laughed, promising she would, without giving the matter much thought.

On Thursday, after Ian had gone and Macadam was back in the office, the rest of the week passed slowly. She was surprised to find she missed Ian's cheerful presence, especially when Macadam was out a lot. Macadam seemed to have recovered from his illness very quickly, although he was still rather pale and drawn.

'Wouldn't it be more sensible if you finished earlier until you've completely recovered your strength?' she suggested, as she put on her coat on on the Friday evening. It was after six and he showed no sign of leaving.

'I may as well stay here as go home to an empty house,' he replied curtly, without looking up.

Staring at his bent head, Zoe wished she could do something to alleviate his loneliness, for he must often feel lonely in that big house on his own. He had friends, but there were times when one needed something more.

'You wouldn't . . . that is . . .' she stammered, and hesitated, her small face flushed from the idea which had just crossed her mind.

'Zoe!' he exclaimed irritably, focussing his attention on her at last, 'will you stop hopping from one leg to the other like a startled stork and get out of here, please?'

Controlling her own quick temper, she smiled at him, albeit nervously. 'I was just going to ask if you'd care to come home with me, Macadam. Gran is making one of her special steak and kidney puddings. I know it might sound a bit much after you've been ill, but honestly, they're as light as a feather, and she always makes too much, because she says she can't make a proper one unless she has a good piece of steak.'

Zoe was quite breathless by the time she had finished, but heard herself adding for good measure, 'It's either that or you go home to an empty house, and no supper!'

'Or I could give Miss Vintis a ring and dine out at one of the big hotels.'

Her face paling, Zoe turned away from his mocking glance. Humiliating tears stung her eyes so she could scarcely see. 'I'm sorry,' she whispered, 'it was silly of me to suggest it. Goodnight.'

Before she had taken two steps Macadam caught up with her. 'Zoe,' he said huskily, 'I'm sorry, I didn't mean that.' Putting his hands on her shoulders, he gently turned her round, grimly noting the tears on her cheeks. 'Forgive me,' he exclaimed gravely, suddenly pulling her to him. 'Of course I'd love to accept your invitation. Sometimes I get tired, you don't know how tired, of my solitary meals and my own company. If you're sure your grandmother won't mind?'

Zoe shook her head. 'I told her you'd been ill, but even if you hadn't been you know she always loves to see you.'

'Which is more than you do.'

Scrubbing at her eyes, Zoe buried her head against Macadam's broad chest, then pulled firmly away from him before he could feel the way her heart was beating wildly. 'I'm usually pleased to see you,' she murmured sedately, without looking at him. Why had she said that—and so coldly, when she knew the days she didn't see him were curiously meaningless.

'Zoe——' he began suddenly, then paused, as though the impulse to speak of something had passed. 'Oh, nothing,' he said curtly, beginning to tidy his desk, pushing a set of keys towards her as she glanced at him expectantly, 'Run down and wait in the car, I'll be with you in a few minutes.'

Her grandparents' house wasn't very fine. It had belonged to Taggart's father, and while he had managed to enlarge it a little and kept it in good order, it was nowhere near the size of Macadam's.

Nevertheless, Zoe saw with a warm rush of pride that it was comfortable and reasonably well furnished. It contained three bedrooms and a bathroom upstairs and on the ground floor a large kitchen-dining-room and a cosy lounge on the other side of the small hall. When they arrived Taggart was reading in the lounge while Janet was busy in the kitchen. She glanced around, her pleasant face beaming with delight when she saw who Zoe had with her.

'Why, come away in, Mr Macadam,' she said in her soft voice, as Zoe explained briefly. 'You're very welcome.'

'Zoe insisted,' he smiled wryly. 'I hope I won't be too much trouble?'

'Of course not,' Janet laughed, adding more soberly, 'She was telling us, only this morning, how ill you've been, and I hope you're feeling better.' When he nodded she suggested, 'Why don't you join Taggart in the lounge while Zoe freshens up and helps me in here?'

Half an hour later they were all sitting round Janet's polished oak table enjoying a delicious meal. Taggart and Macadam, for once, weren't arguing. All his life Taggart had been a voracious reader, loving all manner of books. Macadam, it appeared, had only just discovered this, and since he was no mean student of literature himself, they were soon deep in discussion. It might not last but, while it did, Zoe almost basked in the relaxed atmosphere and felt very happy.

It wasn't until much later in the evening, when they were drinking huge cups of tea before a blazing fire in the lounge, that a hint of the old familiar tension crept in. As Macadam complimented Janet on her mouth-watering home-made biscuits, she asked innocently how he had managed when he was ill.

'Zoe kept popping in and out,' he smiled. 'She looked after me very well indeed.'

Taggart frowned, exclaiming, before Zoe could intercede, 'You mean you were up there together alone?'

'I was ill,' Macadem looked at the old man, his eyes

hardening. 'And even if I hadn't been, what harm would I have done her?'

'Ill? Huh!' Taggart's loud exclamation spoke volumes more than a mere couple of words. He might well have said, when did that ever stop you? That he was quiet merely proved he considered Macadam a guest in his house and therefore common courtesy demanded some degree of reticence. The smouldering darkness in his eyes, however, indicated that Macadam hadn't heard the last of it, and with a sigh Macadam rose to his feet.

'I'll see you in the morning, Zoe,' he said, after thanking Taggart and Janet for their hospitality.

'I'll see you out,' she smiled at him deliberately, ignoring her grandfather's protests that he would do so himself.

'What is this?' Macadam glanced at her enquiringly with a mocking glint in his eye, as she marched with him to the door. 'Don't say you're ready to defy him at last—and over me?'

Stubbornly she shook her head, keeping her own eyes averted from his handsome face. 'It's not a case of you and me, and you know it.'

'Something's been badly missing in your education, my child,' he drawled. 'Weren't you ever taught to read between the lines?'

When Macadam talked in riddles she couldn't follow him. If she did work out what he was on about the answer seldom pleased her, so this time she didn't even bother. Instead she answered coolly, 'I'm glad you enjoyed your meal, if nothing else.'

His dark brows rose at her sharp little remark and as if to punish her for it, he grinned cynically. 'I certainly did. In fact so much that I'm tempted to justify Taggart's worst suspicions and round off an extremely pleasant evening in the accepted fashion.' Before she could move she was a helpless captive, with the bruising force of his kiss bending her head back until she feared her neck would snap. Then, as the heat from his skin seemed to burn hers, he was pushing her away, muttering something derisively.

As she stared at him in a daze, pressing white knuckles against swollen lips, he turned to leave her, adding even more mockingly, 'Goodnight, Zoe. Thanks again.'

The following Thursday Ian returned with a full order book. All, apart from one of the people he had seen, had placed orders, and this man who lived in Mexico City had demanded to see Mr Macadam himself.

Macadam, apparently well satisfied with Ian's endeavours, gave him the weekend off to visit his family. Ian thanked him and said he would go the next morning. That evening he was taking Zoe out to dinner.

Zoe didn't really want to go, but suddenly she felt she had to convince herself there were other men in the world besides Macadam. It was important he realised she thought so, too. Since the night he had dined at her grandparents' house, he had practically ignored her. And whenever she recalled the way he had kissed her, she squirmed with humiliation. She must do her utmost to convince him she attached no importance to such an incident. Therefore she made no secret of the fact that she was looking forward greatly to dining with Ian.

Ian left early the following day, and Macadam made no comment when Zoe described the evening she had spent with him in glowing if slightly exaggerated terms. He maintained a stony silence throughout. Not until her forced enthusiasm came to a rather stumbling halt through lack of encouragement did he point out coldly that if Graham believed he had something to celebrate, it might have been more appropriate if he had asked some of the other staff along as well. They all worked as a team and he didn't like anyone forgetting it.

Feeling suitably chastised, Zoe found it difficult to concentrate for the remainder of the afternoon, and was secretly glad it was Friday. Macadam rapped out orders, one after the other, until she was almost exhausted trying to keep up with him, and, when she dared snatch a few minutes to pop out and see how Donald was getting on with the new sloop he was building for a wealthy customer, he came after her, ordering her back to the office so furiously that not even Donald, an employee of long and valued standing, dared intervene.

Before leaving for home that evening, she asked tentatively if he was going sailing on Sunday. He replied curtly, 'Yes, but alone.'

'Why alone?'

'Because I choose to.'

'I wouldn't mind going.' Zoe swallowed her pride, not quite prepared to beg but almost. 'You usually take me.'

'I'm not taking you this time, Zoe.'

Her green eyes widened with bitter despair. 'I suppose you've invited someone else?'

His gaze went over her in a slow, sweeping scrutiny and his mouth was grim. 'No to that, as well,' he returned shortly. 'And, before I do something I might regret, will you please get out of my sight. Anyway,' he eyed her pale face with what sounded very like a sigh of terse frustration, 'the weather promises to be rough.'

Fear caught her sharply by the throat. 'Then you might need help.'

'Zoe!'

She didn't have to be told twice when Macadam used those tones, but she went unwillingly. It was the first time Macadam had actually refused to let her go with him. Of course he did sail on his own, and with other people. She didn't expect or want to go everywhere, but it was the first time she had asked and been refused, without a reasonable explanation. He knew a little weather never put her off, just as he was aware of what they could achieve together, against anything the skies chose to throw down. No, it had to be he didn't want her any more, and her heart ached dully.

On Saturday she helped about the house and did some shopping for Janet and listened to Taggart's growls with only half an ear. She found she was unable to stop thinking of Macadam, her mood fluctuating painfully between anger and despondency. His rejection of her hurt more than she cared to admit, but there seemed nothing she could do about it. Eventually, to escape her own thoughts, she went for a walk along the sea front, watching the occasional lone yacht out in the bay and the big MacBrayne steamers coming in. Afterwards, on the High Street, she bumped into Freddy Vintis, and while she was talking to him Macadam passed them. He didn't stop. He merely glanced at them keenly and raised his hand in silent acknowledgement.

'What's the matter with him?' Freddy asked. 'He doesn't seem any too sociable. I wanted a word with him.'

'He's been ill.' As usual, Zoe found herself defending Macadam quickly. It didn't strike her as being somewhat inconsistent, that while she might mentally tear him to pieces herself, she couldn't bear hearing even a hint of criticism from anyone else.

Freddy was willing enough to accept her explanation and asked her if she wouldn't like to have a cup of tea. He had been to London, which was why he hadn't given her a ring. He was, apparently, a kind of sleeping partner in a business which had suddenly developed troubles.

Zoe did consent to have tea with him, but when he invited her to go out driving with him the next day she managed to produce a feeble excuse.

'I usually spend Sunday with my grandparents,' she said, and though he frowned he didn't argue.

'I'll give you a ring next week, then,' he said, 'and this time I mean it.'

On Sunday, after lunch, she went along to the boat-yard to see if she couldn't persuade Macadam to change his mind about taking her sailing with him. She wasn't sure what kind of reception she would receive, but suddenly she didn't care. He could only say no again and he might, just conceivably, say yes. She had actually told Janet she was going out with him and didn't know what she would do if he was still in the same mood as he had been on Friday, and refused.

She almost ran the last few yards when she saw he had a boat already prepared to leave. Her anxiety only diminished as she noticed the office door was open and realised he must still be there, probably gathering some gear together. Taking a deep breath, she ran up the stairs to his office and found him.

He glanced up from his desk, his face hardening as he saw who it was. 'No, Zoe!' he snapped, before she could even open her mouth. 'You already have my answer. Now scram, I have a phone call to make.'

Turning his broad back on her, he began dialling, and suddenly her mind was made up. Allowing an anguished little cry to escape her lips, to give the impression that she was beaten and knew it, she ran swiftly downstairs again. Without allowing herself to hesitate she took a flying leap on to his boat and almost dived down below.

CHAPTER FIVE

In the small cabin Zoe quickly wedged herself into the first small space she found, completely out of sight. She was glad she wasn't very big and she hoped Macadam wouldn't discover she was on board until they were well away from the harbour. If he didn't find out until then he might just possibly relent and let her stay with him for the rest of the day.

After a few minutes she heard him arrive and the engines start up. He must be going out under steam, in a hurry. The weather didn't look too good, it was squally but warm—too warm, she thought with a frown, for the time of year. Macadam knew what he was doing, though, he never took unnecessary risks. Slowly Zoe relaxed and before she knew what was happening, she was asleep.

She had intended, originally, to stay where she was, if Macadam remained unaware of her presence for an hour or two, so, even if he was furious and took her straight back, she would at least have time to enjoy a short sail. She slept, however, much longer than she had planned and woke with a start, and a feeling that something was desperately wrong.

The boat was pitching terribly, and she needed only a second to realise they were in the middle of a storm. The wind was coming in violent gusts, and after a loud peal of thunder, lightning flashed vividly and alarmingly through the cabin. Outside, she could hear the shriek of wind in the rigging and the furious crashing of waves breaking around them.

Where was Macadam? Suddenly she found herself shaking with fear, not for her own safety but for his.

She knew a sudden storm could catch even the most experienced seaman unawares. In most instances it was perfectly possible to survive under such conditions, she and Macadam had done it before, and she had learnt to keep a healthy fear of the elements in its proper perspective. Right now it was the uncanny quiet on the boat which made her shiver. It was incredible, yet in the midst of the storm she was conscious of a deathly silence, which seemed unnatural. Something had happened to Macadam, she knew instinctively. And, in the same instant, as a terrible apprehension swept over her, she realised she loved him.

A revelation like this had to be digested slowly, but circumstances forced Zoe to put it immediately aside. Macadam's life could depend on it. The yacht was only thirty feet long, but she was built on sturdy lines, her sails capable of dealing with heavy weather. The last time Zoe and Macadam had been hit by a storm they had lowered all sail and turned into the wind, with several warp lines trailing out at stern which had helped break the crest of the following waves, stopping them from crashing over the boat. Macadam had also shored up the hatch and lashed them both into the cockpit. That had been off Orkney, in the Pentland Firth, notorious for its rough seas. And while procedure might differ, depending on many things which included currents, tides, their exact position and the severity of the weather, she was sure if Macadam had been all right she would have heard him moving about.

He could be in the cockpit, of course. This hope did cross her mind while fear galvanised her to swift action. Quickly she threw on waterproof oilskins and safety harness, intending on deck to attach the stout line on the belt to a lifeline, to prevent herself being swept overboard.

Carefully containing her impatience, knowing one

wrong move might be fatal, she scrambled out of the cabin. Immediately the force of the gale hit her and to her horror she saw the worst of her fears realised as she almost fell over Macadam, lying helpless at her feet.

With quick comprehension, she guessed what had happened. They must have dipped into a huge wave and the strain had somehow snapped the mast, catching him a glancing blow on the side of the head. He was unconscious and before her horrified eyes was sliding slowly away from her, down the deck. He wore safety harness, but it wasn't attached to anything. Unable to reach him, she watched with a kind of paralysed helplessness, expecting to see him swept immediately into the boiling, turbulent seas.

Then suddenly the vessel keeled over, throwing him back towards her again. Struggling desperately to keep her feet on the wet, heaving boards, she grasped him, clipping him automatically to a lifeline, while a mountainous wave flooded the boat from bow to stern. It seemed a miracle that they didn't turn over completely.

Feeling half drowned, Zoe brushed the water and hair from out her eyes and began pulling Macadam into the cockpit. She might not have succeeded in getting him there if the roll of the boat hadn't helped her. He was so heavy she might not have been able to move him more than inches. As it was, terror lent her strength and the tilt of the boat did the rest.

Once inside she released a sobbing breath, then tied them both in, as Macadam had done in the Pentland Firth. She didn't realise she was acting instinctively, basing her every movement on what he had taught her. If she had a conscious thought in her head it was to put her arms round him, to hold him close and protect him. But there were other things to do, things which she fancied she heard him telling her were more important, if they were to survive at all.

After seeing he was fairly comfortable, she glanced at the wound on his head more closely. It looked superficial—she prayed it was, and that he might not be long in recovering consciousness. In the meantime she knew it was up to her to do what she could to keep them afloat, if it was possible.

She tried the engine, but it didn't respond. Something must be badly wrong, she decided. She wasn't sure where they were. Drifting somewhere off Mull, she thought, probably down the coast. They could be anywhere. Along the coast there were numerous small, uninhabited islands, some of them little more than patches of land or chunks of rock rearing out of the sea, a sanctuary for seals and wild-life. Tourists on the big steamers, viewed them with pleasure, but for the lone yachtsman in a storm, they became only an additional hazard.

Again she tried the engine. This time the starter worked, but the engine wouldn't. With a sigh she put the key in her pocket as a safety precaution. In normal circumstances they would have dropped anchor and done a careful check. As it was, she was helpless to do anything. She could only stand by and watch while the boat drifted, entirely at the mercy of the raging seas.

If the engine had been working she might have been able to reduce their speed and control their movements better. As it was, she could only do her best to keep on what she hoped was a steady course and pray the steering didn't fail. She had managed to get a little brandy into Macadam, but as yet he showed no signs of coming round.

It seemed ironical that just as he did the island loomed up before them. Zoe had felt the tug of undercurrents and the boat had nearly heeled over twice. The island wasn't exactly a surprise as she sensed the sudden extra turbulence was caused by the tide flooding into a bay while a wind was blowing offshore. All the same, with the sure knowledge of what might happen, despite her endeavours to be calm, she felt terror rising in her throat to almost choke her. Through the wildness of storm-driven spray and churning waves, she caught odd glimpses of rocks but could discern no beach. And, even if there was one, a boat driven on to it in these conditions might easily capsize, and if it did how was she to get Macadam out? Never before had Zoe known such terrible despair, she could have screamed from the anguished pain of it. If Macadam died, she might as well die, too, she decided. Without him life wouldn't be worth living.

Her relief when he opened his eyes was so great she couldn't speak. Tears blinding her, she gazed at him, her mouth working, but no sound coming through her trembling lips. 'Macadam!' she whispered hoarsely, at last. 'Oh, thank God!'

'Zoe?' He was staring at her as though he was seeing a ghost. 'Where are we?' he exclaimed, struggling to get up.

Now she couldn't speak quickly enough. 'You had an accident, you've been unconscious. The engine's useless and we're about to be beached.'

She didn't need to tell him twice, nor did he waste time asking questions which would keep. Taking one look at the swollen masses of sea surrounding them, he began issuing terse but welcome instructions. In a matter of seconds, it seemed, they were both wearing lifebelts and he had taken every precaution he could to meet such an emergency. When their keel hit the bottom they were prepared for it, although there wasn't a great deal they could do. The yacht shuddered as she was caught on the shingle and the green, turbulent waters receded, leaving her stranded, if still some yards from the water's edge.

They hadn't been completely wrecked, as Zoe had

feared they might be, but they were still in some danger. She realised this, even before Macadam told her. Afterwards she was never able to recall anything in any detail, possibly because so many factors contributed to confuse her—the noise of the sea, the flying spray off mountainous waves, the rain sheeting down with the wind blowing everything about them, taking away all sense of reality. When she moved it was more by instinct now than by rational thought.

Macadam had always said no one should ever abandon a ship while she was still in one piece, and Zoe wondered if he meant to remain on board. In this case it soon became evident he did not. His head must have been hurting, but he appeared to ignore it as he struggled desperately, but with cool precision, to get them out of the danger they were in. Zoe stumbled, knocking her own head as her feet slithered on the streaming decks, but managed to obey him blindly when he shouted something about the dinghy being their only hope. She was scarcely aware of him dragging her overboard or of being mercifully swept ashore.

It wasn't quite as easy as that. She thought a wave tipped the dinghy over and Macadam grabbed hold of her, swimming the last few yards to dry land. It seemed a miracle, under such conditions, that they ever reached it, and if it hadn't been for Macadam she knew she could never have made it alone.

She wasn't sure whether she lost complete consciousness or not, but she was aware of nothing more until she realised he was bending over her, pumping the water from her lungs.

'Reece!' she protested, the salt in her mouth making her feel sick, while the pressure of his hands hurt. Slowly she sat up, then suddenly stared at him. His face was as pale as her own and haggard, but he actually smiled. 'What's so funny?' she gasped.

'You—calling me Reece,' he replied oddly. 'I

thought you never would. It's taken a storm, a ship-wreck—our lives, almost.'

She went on staring at him, wanting to tell him he was right in a way but only partly so. It had taken a storm to make her realise she loved him, that she had loved him for a long time and never known. With a flicker of her lashes she lowered her eyes, for fear he should guess. 'I didn't realise,' she muttered, changing the subject quickly, without giving him a chance to pursue it. 'I got a bump on the head, remember, the same as you.'

His smile faded as he nodded guardedly, his hands going lightly to her face. 'Do you feel all right?' he asked abruptly.

'I'm all right,' her eyes flew back to his anxiously, 'but are you?' As he nodded again she went even paler, recalling how she had found him. 'Are you sure?' she insisted. 'I got a terrible fright. I thought I was going to lose you. What happened?'

'I hit a trough, or it could have been the lightning—I don't seem to remember very clearly. The last thing I knew was hitting the deck. I believe you must have saved my life.'

'And you mine,' she said quickly. 'I could never have got ashore on my own.'

As the force of the gale whipped her words away he frowned, glancing about him, as if reminded they were still in considerable danger, if only from exposure.

'Do you know where we are?' Zoe asked, as this suddenly occurred to her as well.

'I can't be certain.' He leaned nearer to make sure she heard. 'I think I do. If I'm not mistaken it's an uninhabited island belonging to a writer who now wants to sell it. He isn't living here now, but if this is the one, there'll be a house and we'll be in luck!'

Jumping to his feet, he drew her gently up beside him, keeping his arm tightly around her, sheltering her as well as he could from the driving rain. 'Zoe!' he exclaimed softly, bending his head to press his cheek compulsively against her wet one. As his mouth touched her face tenderly she shivered as a sudden ecstasy shot through her.

Mistaking her reaction for coldness, he withdrew. 'Sorry,' he said tersely. 'You can blame the knock on my head. We'd better get to the top of the cliffs and see if I'm right about the island.'

'What about the boat?' she asked, as he turned her towards the steep incline.

Without pausing, he snapped, 'That's not the most important thing at the moment. We're both soaked to the skin and cold. We have to try and find shelter.'

'Couldn't we be on Mull?' She stared up at his grim face enquiringly, wondering where all his tenderness had gone.

'Not a chance,' he pulled her closer again, guiding her round a rocky boulder, 'I was too far away when the storm broke.'

Above their heads a seabird called, a wild, lonely sound on the wind. Zoe couldn't stop thinking about the boat, knowing how much it had meant to Reece. 'Will it ever sail again?' she muttered, almost to herself.

Impatiently, he sighed. 'I managed to throw an anchor overboard, which might hold her, providing the weather doesn't get worse, but, as I've already said, she isn't the most important consideration. We have to find this chap's house.'

'Are you sure you're strong enough to walk that far?'

'Why so worried?' he said dryly, as though remembering her rejection of his kiss. 'I'm okay. My head's aching a bit,' he admitted, 'but I don't suppose I'll feel any better until I get inside, somewhere.' As she slipped on the wet shingle, his arm tightened until she regained her balance. 'Stop arguing,' he commanded. 'You've had just about as much as you can take. Let's just concentrate on getting up this path.'

The incline wasn't nearly so steep as it had looked from the beach and it became obvious, despite the weather, that the path had been fairly well used. As they successfully negotiated the last few yards of it, a house loomed in view. It wasn't so much a house as a tumbledown cottage, but Zoe loved it on sight. It looked to be about half a mile away.

'Oh, isn't it beautiful!' she exclaimed, tears in her eyes.

Reece grinned wryly, 'I know exactly how you feel.'

She doubted it, but merely shook her head. All sorts of strange feelings were sweeping over her. She loved him and it was wonderful to know they were safe. That he was safe. She didn't think she would ever forget that terrible moment on the yacht when she had watched him sliding away from her. But she wouldn't think of it now. In front of them was a cottage, shelter—a refuge from the storm. Wasn't this enough to be going on with?

'Aren't you going to race me, Reece?' she smiled at him, suddenly so radiant, he blinked with astonishment.

'No, definitely not,' he teased, his blue eyes laughing. 'I'd probably fall flat on my face in the first few yards, and you'd never let me live it down.'

Surprisingly it was Zoe who proved to have the least strength. Her legs turning suddenly shaky, she stumbled so much that eventually Reece picked her up and carried her all the way to the house. Despite her protests, he refused to put her down until they reached it.

'You implied you were the weak one,' she whispered unevenly, as he dropped her gently to her feet.

'It must have been the way you smiled at me,' he replied.

The door was closed but not locked. Inside it was clean but spartan, reminding Zoe very much of the cottage where the otter and his master had lived in *Ring Of Bright Water*. There appeared to be only one room, containing a rough bed squeezed into one corner. In front of the open hearth stood a sturdy table, while makeshift bookshelves lined the walls, packed with an assortment of dusty books.

'A poor place but mine own,' Reece misquoted softly, drawing Zoe inside and closing the door.

'Did he really live here? The writer, I mean,' she asked, still gazing around curiously.

'Five years, I believe.' Reece tossed the wet hair from his eyes, brushing it back with an impatient hand as he began piling wood on the hearth. 'He was studying the seals and birds, then suddenly decided he'd had enough.'

'He must be a very good sort, all the same,' she commented appreciatively, 'to have left all that dry wood.'

'I wasn't criticising him.' Reece glanced, with a hint of amusement, at her indignant face. 'I'm really very grateful that his house is here and available. As for the wood, people living on islands often make a habit of collecting it, driftwood, washed up on the shore. As we were,' he muttered more harshly.

Zoe found she was shivering, both from his tone of voice and the cold. 'Have we any matches?' she asked, realising with dismay that they might not have anything to light a fire.

'I have a waterproof packet on me.' Reece threw off his soaked jacket to enable him to get at them. As the flames leapt to an almost instant heat, he gave a grunt of satisfaction and added more wood. Turning to Zoe again, he said curtly, 'Better start getting out of those wet clothes, unless you want to catch pneumonia.'

Flushing slightly, she glanced at him quickly. 'Is there anything we could wear, do you think, while our own clothes are drying?'

His mouth twisted. 'I see what you mean. I'll have a look.' He opened the door of an old cupboard and she was relieved to see it contained an assortment of garments.

'A shirt, anyway,' he threw it to her. 'It looks big enough to cover you completely. There's a pair of pants which might do for me. I can't seem to see another shirt, so I'll have to do without until mine dries. Good job there's a difference in our anatomy.'

As he withdrew his head from the cupboard, the colour in Zoe's cheeks deepened. 'We only have one room.'

Reece eyed her sardonically. 'I'm afraid I can't do anything about that, but we can always turn our backs on each other.' Mockingly, as though to punish her lack of trust, he added, 'If we must.'

What he meant was, if she must. Suddenly, as a feeling of recklessness swept over her, Zoe found herself railing against the conventions she had observed all her life. Reece was right to mock. What place had foolish, silly pride in a situation like this? They were both cold, almost ill with it, despite their joint efforts to make light of it. If she distrusted Reece enough to believe he was about to rape her at any moment, then she didn't deserve his respect.

'It doesn't matter,' she bent her head so he shouldn't notice her regrettable embarrassment. 'That was stupid of me, after all we've been through.'

'Yes,' he agreed, but as though he didn't attach much importance to it. Hastily she began struggling with buttons.

'Here, let me,' he went to her assistance almost indifferently. 'Oilskins can be very unwieldy.' Removing the coat from her slim shoulders, he threw it aside. 'That didn't keep you very dry, did it?'

Ruefully she glanced at it. 'I don't think anything would withstand total submersion!'

Her thick sweater came next, then her shirt and jeans, all the time Reece working methodically, no expression on his face. Her jeans caused the most trouble. Through being wet, they were too tight and there were patches of red on her long, slender legs before he managed to get her out of them. When at last she stood in only her scanty bra and panties, he picked up the shirt and passed it to her.

'You'd better do the rest yourself, Zoe, I think.'

She could tell nothing of what he was thinking. There was only a faint tinge of red over his cheekbones which she put down to exertion. Quickly she slipped the shirt over her head, wriggling out of her underclothing beneath its protective folds. 'Your friend must be a giant!' she smiled.

'Yes,' Reece turned his attention to his own wet clothes, 'he's tall, anyway.'

While he changed she saw to the fire and when she looked up again she noticed his pants fitted him very well, apart from around the waist where they were a little on the big side.

'There's a kettle,' he said, 'and, I think, a spring at the door. While I go and fetch some water, be a good girl and see if you can find some coffee or tea.'

Feeling awkward in her long shirt and bare feet, Zoe opened the door of another cupboard which she hoped might hold such things. Now she was dry and warmer, she felt much happier. She even began to feel a sense of adventure, which seemed surprising, after what they'd been through.

She didn't find any coffee, but there was half a packet of teabags and a tin of milk. As they waited for the kettle to boil she discovered some tins of baked beans and biscuits, along with some sugar. 'At least we won't starve,' she said, showing them to Reece.

'We'd better open one tin at a time,' he said. 'We don't know how long they may have to last.'

About to pass him a tin-opener, Zoe paused. She had been absorbed with other things, but it was still incredible that she hadn't given a thought as to how they were to get away from here. Or about the people at home.

'Do you think we'll have to stay until the storm passes over?' she asked.

Glancing at her quickly, he replied bluntly, 'We'll probably have to stay here all night. In the morning I'll take a look at the boat, if she's still there, but I can't promise anything until I see what kind of condition she's in.'

'I see.' Zoe's forehead creased anxiously. 'And what about letting anyone know where we are? My grandparents are bound to be terribly worried.'

'It's a pity you didn't think of that sooner,' he remarked acidly. 'It's not my fault they won't know you're with me.'

It was the first time he had mentioned it and she had the grace to look ashamed. 'I—— I told Gran I was going with you. I hoped you might change your mind, you see.'

'But I didn't.'

'No.' She pushed the tin and opener towards him before she dared meet his narrowed eyes and answer his unspoken question. 'When you refused the second time, I was so mad I didn't stop to think. I hid on board while you were making your phone call and fell asleep.'

'I thought something like that must have happened.' Reece tipped the beans in a pan, placing it on a hob near the fire. As he turned back to her, his face was grim. 'You always were a spoiled little brat, Zoe. If I'd known what you were up to you wouldn't have been able to sit down for a week!'

'All the same,' she muttered stubbornly, while her pulse raced with fright, 'I don't regret what I did. You can pretend to hate me, but you know you would have been drowned if it hadn't been for me. I had an awful struggle to get you off the deck. Not that I expect gratitude . . .'

'You aren't getting any,' he said coldly. 'No amount of whining or effusive speechifying is going to solve our immediate problem, my girl. The fact remains that because of your stupid inability to take no for an answer, your grandparents are in for a very anxious time. It's too dark and wild to even try to get to the yacht to send a message tonight.'

Glancing through the window, Zoe didn't argue. The storm had scarcely abated and she was aware of despair and pain because of the things he had said to her. Home-truths were seldom easy to listen to, but it was the dislike in Reece's voice when he spoke to her which she found hardest to bear.

'If you hadn't come I might have been dead,' he said coldly, 'but no one would have been unduly worried.'

'That's a beastly thing to say!' she choked, her face going white, her head reeling.

His mouth merely twisted cynically. 'Your concern might be touching, darling, if I thought it was genuine. Now, I think we'd better eat our supper and go to bed, and see what tomorrow brings.'

He had taken aspirin and insisted his head was none the worse. He was irritated when she kept on enquiring about it, so she decided to do as she was told. The beans tasted good and the biscuits, washed down with cups of hot, sweet tea, provided a fairly adequate finale to their meal. Reece ate and drank more than Zoe. Knowing how worried Janet and Taggart would be took away most of her appetite. Reece's attitude didn't help either. Meeting the disapproval in his eyes, as they sat together at the small table, she wondered bleakly how she had ever come to imagine she loved him.

'Isn't there any other way of getting word?' she asked eventually.

She didn't have to explain what she was talking about. 'If there was do you think I wouldn't try?' he said tersely.

'I don't know,' she muttered distractedly. As his face darkened, she hurried on, 'Yes, I'm sure you would, but I was thinking more of the island than the boat. Are you sure it's uninhabited? Just supposing you'd made a mistake and there were other houses?'

Grimly, he shook his head. 'I'm quite certain I have my facts right, and if I did go and search to make absolutely sure, in the dark what could I see? On unfamiliar ground it could be madness—I might easily fall into a bog or over a cliff.' He shrugged, as if to say as far as he was concerned it wouldn't matter, but he asked, his eyes glinting, 'How would you manage if I did? Left here on your own, it could be weeks, even months before you were found.'

Shivering, on both counts, Zoe attempted to apologise. 'I'm sorry, Reece. There must be something the matter with my head.'

'I'm afraid I'm inclined to agree.' Grimly he rose to his feet and began to clear the table.

Zoe watched dully as he gathered up the pan and cups, putting everything in a large plastic dish and pouring over them the last of the hot water in the kettle. Somehow she hadn't the heart to help. While they'd eaten supper, Reece had aired the blankets off the bed beside the fire. After finishing the dishes he remade it, remarking, with some satisfaction, that both the bed and the blankets were quite dry.

Coolly, when he had completed this task, he commanded, 'Come and get in, while I make up the fire. I'll probably wait until you're asleep before I join you.'

'Join me?' Zoe was shocked out of her apathy. Childishly she exclaimed, 'We can't share a bed, we aren't married!'

With a harsh expletive, he turned on her angrily. 'Have you no sense? It's a case of survival, keeping warm. Or would you rather take turns? I'll sit by the fire for a few hours, then we can change over.'

Zoe stared at him, her small face hot with frustration. If she refused to sleep with him it would imply that she believed he would take advantage of the situation, yet, if she agreed, how was she to feel when they were in bed together?

As something of her indecision showed, he observed mockingly, 'You still don't trust me, Zoe?'

Suddenly it all proved too much for her. She averted her head, but not before he had seen the tears rolling down her flushed cheeks. With a muffled groan he reached out, drawing her to him.

As his arms went closely around her trembling body, through the thin cotton of her shirt she could feel the warmth and hardness of him flowing into her like a burning tide. When his lips crushed hers, swiftly and passionately, she responded unthinkingly, feeling unable to move, let alone struggle. Dazedly she wondered if this was a kind of punishment for her contrariness as the kiss went on and on, as if he was seeking out every bit of rebellion in her, draining her lips of the last bit of resistance until she could hardly breathe.

'Zoe,' he muttered, in a kind of savage voice, thick with urgency, 'you know I wouldn't hurt you, but you make it damned difficult—the things you say. Even what you merely think!'

'I'm sorry,' she murmured, clinging to him, not

really aware of anything, uncaring if she was hurt.

He caressed her check gently with long fingers. She could feel the roughness of his chest almost bruising her breasts. The belt of his pants pressed into her stomach and the muscles of his strong legs were rigid against the softer slenderness of her own. Vaguely she realised he was exercising great self-control.

'I'm sorry, too,' he replied slowly. 'I owe you a lot for saving my life. I won't forget.'

'I don't want you to remember it as a debt.' She let one slim hand travel experimentally over his shoulders. His skin was warm, slightly roughened, but she had an irresistible desire to touch her mouth to it.

'A debt is a debt,' he murmured, almost as if he wasn't thinking of what he was saying but intent on the course her hand was taking. Then with a sound which was halfway between a sigh and groan he bent to her again. Their mouths met and clung and she felt helpless to deny the wild flood of response he aroused in her, for all she tried to resist it. Her arms locked around his neck, which was smooth and strong like his shoulders. Fiercely she pressed against him, murmuring his name, until the sound of it, mingling with the accelerating beat of her heart, threatened to send her into a kind of frantic delirium. As he kissed her eyes, her cheeks and her hair, she offered up her mouth again with a complete lack of pretence or restraint.

Then his head jerked, like a man sensing danger, and he stopped. Suddenly he was picking her up, ignoring her trembling lips as he carried her to the bed. Tersely he said, 'I think it's time you got some rest.'

Though it might be what she needed, it was the last thing she wanted. As he laid her down, none too gently, she clutched at him tightly. 'Kiss me goodnight, Reece,' she begged, refusing to be ashamed. 'I—— I would like you to.'

Her husky confession didn't have the desired effect. His face shuttered and dark, he exclaimed, 'Must you be so brazen? What you really want is a rude awakening! You're like a child crying for candy, and you aren't getting any!'

Instantly driven, as always, by the hurt of his rejection, Zoe cried defiantly, 'Want to bet?'

The mounting fury, almost leaping from his glittering eyes, removed her fleeting bravado. Without waiting for his verbal reply, she turned over, burying her hot face in the cool pillow. If Reece had anything to say, and she could guess the nature of any further comment, she had no wish to hear it.

She was so tired that despite what had just taken place she thought she would have dropped off at once, but curiously she found sleep evaded her. Her eyes kept opening, straying towards Reece as he sat by the fire, clinging to him as if she had never seen him before. Was it only because she imagined she loved him that he had turned into an exciting stranger?

Stirring uneasily, she decided she was possibly deluding herself. What they had been through together had obviously heightened her emotions to a pitch where love and desire became so interwoven it was impossible to tell one from the other. Perhaps Reece was right when he said she was like a child crying for candy. If she had any sense at all she would forget the way in which his kisses had affected her and go to sleep.

CHAPTER SIX

ZOE was still trying to deal firmly with her irrational emotions when she saw Reece get wearily to his feet and look across at her. Immediately she pretended to be asleep. After a moment's hesitation, during which he must have decided she was, he came to the bed and stretched out beside her. Lifting the rumpled surplus of the blanket covering her, he pulled it over himself with an impatient sigh. As Zoe held her breath, something difficult to achieve, the way her heart was pounding, he turned on to his back, lacing his hands behind his head.

Why had he put them there? Was it to keep them out of mischief? she wondered, her mouth quirking wryly at the unusual trend of her thoughts. Then she remembered her grandfather, visualising his anger if he could see her now. Not surprisingly every vestige of humour fled as a quiver of apprehension rushed over her.

Instinctively seeking protection, as she had done many times before, she turned to Reece nervously, with a half smothered cry. 'He'd kill me!' she muttered indistinctly.

Swiftly, with a soft word of comfort, Reece took his hands from his head to take hold of her. Gently he drew her nearer to him, obviously believing she was having a bad dream.

Zoe stopped thinking of her grandfather. Feeling Reece's arms around her, she snuggled shamelessly closer. Something told her such an incident might not happen again and she wanted to savour every moment of it. 'Reece,' she murmured, drowsily content.

At once he stiffened. 'I thought you were asleep.'

'Does it matter?' she sighed.

He didn't move, but she felt him tense. 'Why aren't you asleep?' he persisted.

'How should I know?' she replied absently, rubbing a soft hand against him, meaning to appease. As she touched him his muscles went rigid under her tentative fingers. There was the slight tang of salt tantalising her delicate nostrils. 'It must be the seawater,' she whispered shakily, breathing it in.

'Zoe! What on earth are you on about now?' he snapped.

'Your skin, it smells salty,' she tried to explain.

'So does yours. And we will, until we get back to civilisation and have a bath,' he said curtly.

'I wasn't complaining. It's not unpleasant,' she said softly.

Tilting her head a little, she saw he was watching her coldly, although he made no attempt this time to push her away. He was impervious, she realised hollowly. He might have kissed her before and enjoyed it, but she suspected his greatest pleasure had lain in the alleviation of his feelings. Previously when he had kissed her it had been his frustrated way of settling an argument or his anger. Being a particularly dominant male he had no compunction about using his superior strength to help him win a verbal battle. Hadn't he always used brute force against her when all else failed? Suddenly she wondered curiously if he would ever be tempted to kiss her for any other reason. Proximity, perhaps, or just plain provocation? Aware that he had enough control to ignore either, Zoe sighed restlessly. Under all her speculation was the uneasy feeling that she was playing with fire, yet she felt she must do something to take her mind off the predicament she was in. That they were comparatively safe after being shipwrecked did nothing to lessen the remorse which consumed her when she thought of the anguish she must be causing back home. Or her dread of her grandfather's fury when she returned.

Half desperately, unconsciously seeking escape from such thoughts, she moved her hands blindly over Reece's broad chest. The fine hairs were rough against her palms and she was startled at the way her skin tingled.

'You know what you're inviting?'

His cool, hard voice made her flinch. There wasn't a hint of tenderness in it anywhere. Resentment welled, but she managed to subdue it, sticking to her resolve not to arouse his anger. Stifling a sigh, she concluded that it was the only thing about him she could arouse easily.

'I've never been in bed with a man before,' she said mutinously. 'You have to make allowances.'

'You aren't exactly in bed with me,' he retorted dryly, 'not in the sense you mean.'

'I suppose not,' she agreed, trying to lighten the situation with a touch of impulsive, if misplaced humour. 'But I might be one day, if I ever get married.'

'You silly child!' he exclaimed roughly. 'Do you imagine Ian Graham or Freddy Vintis, or whoever's bride you intend to be, would care to be presented with a certificate of bedworthiness signed by me?'

He sounded not just angry but furious, something Zoe had wanted to prevent at all cost. 'I wasn't suggesting anything like that!' she cried indignantly.

'And I'm suggesting you don't know what you're talking about, darling. There are certain situations where the lines are so finely drawn it's difficult to remember they even exist.'

He was being nasty again. He only called her darling when she irritated him beyond endurance. Her pulses fluttered as she wondered how she might coax him back to a better mood. His face was close to hers and she gazed at him anxiously. Then, because she couldn't think of anything else, she leaned forward a little and gently kissed him.

It was awkward, because he didn't move his head and her lips merely grazed the corner of his mouth. She was conscious of a sense of frustration when he tensed at her touch, while his eyes mocked her failure to convey anything but her own total lack of expertise. There was no mistaking his awareness of her innocence in the derisive glance he swept over her, and her face burned with humiliation. Anger joined the other turbulent emotions inside her. While men might scorn experience in a girl, they appeared to dislike inexperience even more!

'I hate you!' she cried, her eyes blurred with angry tears.

'Is this something new?' he asked in bored tones. 'You've hated me on and off for years.'

'I've never realised how stuffy you were before!' she muttered recklessly. 'What women see in you I just don't know!'

'Perhaps I should show you?' Reece taunted grimly.

Absorbed in her muddled thoughts, Zoe had temporarily forgotten he could be goaded too far. Used to a lashing from his tongue or occasionally a good shake, she was unprepared for a different kind of reaction. When he grabbed hold of her chin and his mouth descended in a kiss of extreme violence, she was nearly shocked out of her mind.

'No!' she exclaimed, thinking wildly that the impact of his mouth must have marked her for ever.

'You had sufficient warning,' he snapped, carrying on as if she had never spoken.

Zoe's head whirled as his arms tightened, restraining her struggles. She would have welcomed his kisses, along with a few soothing words to supply comfort in a warm, sexless way. The kind of cherishing which might have helped her to relax and drift off to sleep. Reece supplied neither. Whatever he meant to provide it was certainly none of these things.

Always before his caresses had been brief, withdrawn before she had had any real chance to respond, or make sense of her wavering emotions. His approach now was different, utterly sensual. He was sweeping her ruthlessly into realms which she vaguely realised could be dark and dangerous. Because he was furious there was more than a hint of brutality in the way he parted her lips, taking his fill of the soft, innocent sweetness of her mouth.

'Please!' she protested again, gasping.

'No,' he retorted thickly.

She had tried to escape but failed. Now it alarmed her more that she was rapidly losing all desire to do so. Today she had almost drowned in raging seas, now she felt she was drowning in delight. Her blood raced, her heart pounded so she was conscious of little else. Passing through her was a quivering sensation of excitement which left her breathless and bewildered.

When Reece lifted his head and began seeking out the pulsing hollows in her cheeks and throat, she didn't make a sound or movement to resist him. Instead her arms went around his neck, her trembling fingers tangling in the thick darkness of his hair to bring his mouth back to hers again.

Yielding to an overwhelming rapture, she murmured his name, suddenly utterly absorbed yet consumed by an irrational sense of mixed-up urgency. She found herself accepting what was happening as though it was meant to be. She was in Reece's arms, but strangely this wasn't enough. Suddenly she wanted a lot more, and quickly, yet, at the same time, she wanted to savour each moment slowly, to stretch it out so it would last for ever.

He crushed the mouth she offered fiercely, his exploration of it deeper, even more passionate than before. And while he kissed her his hands moved over her restlessly, making no secret of his mounting desire. Lifting himself slightly away from her, he unbuttoned the front of her shirt, then removed it completely to gaze hungrily on her small, high breasts. The pale light from the fire flickering over them appeared to intrigue him. Deliberately his mouth and lean brown fingers touched her white skin, teasing rosy peaks until shattering spears of flame seared right through her and she was tormented by the unsatisfied emotions he aroused.

As her breath came raggedly, he commanded tersely, 'Look at me.'

When she did her eyes were heavy with languor, her mouth bruised and soft, swollen from his passionate kisses. As if satisfied with what he found, he asked huskily, 'Are you still willing to tangle with the unknown?'

Without waiting for an answer, he bent to her again and she watched his face approaching with a kind of dazed wonder, the question he asked barely penetrating the clouded recesses of her mind, or making any sense against the treacherous weakness sweeping her body. As his tongue touched her lips, then parted them, the roughness of his broad chest against the bareness of her own gave the most exquisite pleasure. She was helpless against his strength, or to deny the sweet flood of response his kiss was arousing.

When she whimpered, as the forces within her built up unbearably, his grip merely tightened cruelly until she became utterly pliant in his arms. Then, slowly, his hands slid under her hips, lifting her to him. She was so slender he hurt her, but her body only quivered with a kind of anticipatory fear. She was frightened, but so completely at the mercy of her own passionate nature, and her love for him, that she only wanted to belong to him.

Then, with a startling suddenness, everything changed. 'Zoe?' Reece's voice hit her harshly. 'You're sure you know what you're doing?'

Bewildered, she wondered why he talked as if he wasn't part of it. 'Yes,' she whispered blindly, as yet without shame.

'I'm glad you can be honest about something,' he snapped.

Zoe was stunned at how quickly he removed himself.

'Did you really think I would fall for it?' he exclaimed.

'Fall for what?' She sat up, feeling giddy. What was he talking about?

'A pleasant trap,' he grated, standing contemptuously by the side of the bed. 'You'd like to catch yourself a husband and think I would do!'

Zoe's face went white as for a moment she could scarcely take in what he was saying. When she did, heat coloured her cheeks to a humiliating scarlet. 'You—you believe I was acting deliberately, with that in mind?'

His eyes were fixed on her, as if against his will they refused to leave her. 'The setting was there,' he allowed finally. 'It was probably responsible for giving you the idea. Just be grateful I came to my senses in time, because in another minute it would have been too late.'

Was he trying to tell her something? Angry tears in her eyes, Zoe dismissed it as irrelevant. 'I wouldn't marry you if you were the last person on earth!' she sobbed. 'You've known me all my life and I work or you. I work all hours and would do almost anything for the boatyard and—and the men. And you believe,' she glared at him, trying to hide her despair, 'you believe I've done all this with the sole purpose of trapping you?'

'Would you be content to have an affair with me?' he asked tightly, a white ring round his mouth.

'No!' She was shaking so badly she had difficulty in pulling the blanket over her forgotten nakedness, especially under the insolent surveillance of his narrowed eyes. 'You know I wouldn't,' she cried, yet her voice faltered hoarsely as she wondered if she was speaking the whole truth. Her heart assured her bleakly that one day she might be willing to settle for anything so far as Reece was concerned.

He laughed sardonically, without amusement, 'So— it's neither a husband or an affair? I think you'd better decide what it is you do want before we proceed any further. No one respects a tease.'

Turning from her then, he resumed his former seat by the fire, after picking up her discarded shirt and putting it around his broad shoulders.

Angrily Zoe reflected that it fitted him better than it had done her. He didn't say anything more, nor did she. His actions seemed to speak louder than words. He wanted nothing more to do with her and would spend the rest of the night by the fire, while she had the blanket and the bed. Bitterly she hoped he would enjoy the long, lonely hours as much as she did. Then, wounded beyond belief, she turned her face into the pillow and cried herself silently to sleep.

Her eyes were consequently red and swollen next morning and she guessed she looked a sight. It was barely daylight when she woke with a painful groan to find Reece standing over her.

Staring at her gravely, he handed her a cup of tea. 'How are you feeling, Zoe?' he asked. 'How's the head?'

'I'm fine . . .' Since she couldn't do much about her face she decided to ignore it. As he had already seen it there wasn't much point in doing anything else. Mutinously, as she drank her tea and stretched cramped legs, she wondered how long he had been surveying her before she woke up. She didn't remember mentioning a headache, and if he was offering this a means of saving her pride then he could save his breath! 'There's nothing wrong with my head,' she tilted her softly rounded chin deliberately although she couldn't quite meet his eyes. 'Like the weather, this morning, it seems much clearer.'

'The gale's blown itself out and the clouds are dispersing,' he agreed dryly, turning back to the hearth and his own tea. 'As soon as I've had this I'm going down to the bay to see if the boat is still there.'

'Shall I come with you?' She began scrambling out of bed, then suddenly realised she had nothing on. Flushing with mortification, she was forced to remain where she was.

Reece didn't appear to want more than a brief glimpse of her. Even before she was back under the blanket he had turned away, his face hardening, making her wonder if he imagined she was flaunting herself deliberately again.

When he spoke, however, his voice was grimly expressionless. 'You'd better get dressed while I'm gone. Your clothes are dry.'

'When's breakfast?' she asked, her own voice, by contrast, annoyingly unsteady.

His attention returned to her closely, taking in her pallor, the vulnerable tremor of her defiantly raised chin. His mouth tightened. 'If the yacht's there and I can reach her, there's supplies on board. I'll bring something back.'

'Reece?' she cried urgently, watching him leaving.

'Yes?' He paused enquiringly by the door.

'You will be careful?' she faltered.

'Naturally,' his thick brows lifted as she hesitated, 'And . . .?'

'If she is there, and you do get on board, you won't forget to send a message back home?'

'If the radio's working it's the first thing I'll do,' he promised coldly. 'I suppose that's why you're begging me to be careful?'

After he had gone it took her only a few short minutes to get into her jeans and sweater. She didn't stop to comb her hair or wash her face. She had to go after him. Did he really think it was possible for her to wait here patiently while he might easily be in danger again? When she had mentioned breakfast it had merely been to cover up a sudden dizziness that had assailed her, she had scarcely realised what she was saying. She felt empty, in a strange way, but not hungry.

As she pulled on canvas shoes which were still damp, she wondered if Reece would have left her so easily this morning if his passion had progressed to a natural conclusion during the night. Recalling the strength of his arms, the hard, sensuous warmth of his mouth, she didn't think so. With a painful tremor she realised she might not have been so innocent this morning if—to use his own words—he had not come to his senses in time.

Bitterly she reflected that but for his well developed sense of self-preservation she might still have been in his arms. Perhaps she should be grateful that single men rarely reached his age without becoming extremely wary—of traps! Mirthlessly, Zoe giggled, brushing a few stray tears impatiently from her cheeks. Just who did he think he was? she asked herself angrily.

She knew, of course, as did everyone. Reece came from an illustrious Edinburgh family and would never think seriously about a girl like herself. She could imagine the faces of his relatives if he were to present Zoe Kerr as his future wife. His—future wife . . . She almost laughed aloud. It had never once occurred to her to covet such a position. If it did now, she recognised it as being wholly foolish.

It could only be a matter of time before she was back to normal again. While she might feel very different from the girl she had been yesterday, there was nothing like a glimpse of harsh reality for removing rosy dreams from a girl's eyes. Yesterday she had been convinced she had fallen in love with Reece Macadam. She could only hope desperately he hadn't been aware of that. She must make sure he understood that the shock of being ship-wrecked must have been responsible for the way she had behaved.

When she went outside the air smelled fresh and clean and only a very few clouds disturbed the pale blueness of the skies. The wind had dropped to the light breeze which always seemed to blow over the islands. It was all so quiet and peaceful, it was difficult to believe storms ever happened.

Zoe didn't stop to survey the wild grandeur of her surroundings, as she made her way anxiously across the rough ground to the cliff edge. To her amazement the yacht was still there, looking not much the worse for the battering she had taken, apart from a broken mast. Zoe stared incredulously, for she had secretly feared the boat would be smashed to pieces on the rocks. When Reece had talked of bringing something for their breakfast and she had asked him not to forget to send a message, it had been more, she suspected, of an attempt to keep their spirits up than because of any great belief that it would be possible to do either.

Now, as she saw they might, with luck, be able to leave the island sooner than they had expected, her spirits rose. She didn't care how hard she worked, nothing could be worse than having to stay here with Macadam. As she stayed motionless, for a moment, gazing out over the empty stretch of endless seas, she was grateful that she might be spared the risk of making a fool of herself again.

Macadam wasn't on the shore when she reached it, but when she hailed the boat he appeared on deck. While she waited impatiently, he came to her in the dinghy.

'We're in luck,' he confirmed her hopes with a grin of satisfaction. 'The dinghy was washed up, miraculously, and the old boat's not in bad shape at all. We'll have to work on her, of course, but first, I think, breakfast. Then we needn't stop again until we're ready to go.'

He was talking briskly, obviously intent, Zoe thought, on returning their relationship to its old footing. Feeling it was up to her to at least try to meet him halfway, she swallowed quickly, saying briefly,

'I'm sorry, Macadam, about last night.'

'So,' he stared at her averted face coldly, 'we're back to that, are we?'

'I almost decided not to mention it,' she wished now she hadn't. 'What happened doesn't make me feel very proud of myself.'

'Probably not,' he broke in curtly, 'but I wasn't talking about last night. I was referring to the way you've gone back to using my surname. What's wrong with Reece?'

'Oh,' she attempted to shrug indifferently, 'I hadn't given it a thought.'

'So you haven't really changed?'

Zoe shivered at the chilly glint in his eyes but ploughed on bravely. 'You wouldn't want me to, surely?'

'Zoe!' he snapped tersely, his face pale under his tan, 'I'm asking questions, not answering them.'

'Perhaps I don't feel bright enough to answer anything,' she retorted sullenly. 'We aren't in the office this morning, you know.'

'Just as well.' He took a menacing step towards her.

Her heart beating suddenly faster, she sought urgently for a means of diverting him. 'Is the radio working?' she asked eagerly.

'Yes.' He halted only inches from her, his glance piercing. 'I sent a message that we'd run into some slight difficulties but should be home later today. I didn't go into details as I didn't want to worry your grandparents unduly.'

'Oh, good.' She felt almost lyrical with relief, but sobered quickly again. 'I don't suppose I can ever make up for the anxiety I've caused them, but I'll do my best.'

'Don't labour over it too hard, my child,' he advised sharply. 'Your grandparents were born into seagoing families. They've learnt to live with the elements, and the worry attached. It's a part of our lives.'

'Which is no excuse for worrying them unnecessarily,' Zoe pointed out unhappily.

'Well, resolve not to do it again.' Impatiently Reece noted the tears in her eyes. 'And if you must make a martyr of yourself, don't enjoy it too much.'

'Sometimes I think you're inhuman!' she cried.

He grabbed her by the shoulders angrily. 'Didn't last night prove I'm very human indeed?'

Equally angry, she stared up at him. His fingers bit deeply into her skin and she was lost in the intense blue of his eyes. The fire she thought had died hours ago began rekindling within her, making her head swim. He caught her to him harshly, kissing her ruthlessly, as though demanding submission.

'Let me go!' she gasped, as he paused to draw breath.

'For the moment I will.' He released her as if nothing had happened, but she flinched at the peculiar threat in his voice. Turning from her abruptly, he added stringently, 'We'll have to get on.'

A little later Zoe cooked breakfast on board the yacht, leaving Reece to make a further brief inventory of what must be done before they could sail. He had said that, as the galley was still in one piece, it would be easier to eat on the boat than to carry everything to the cottage. She suspected he was no keener than she was to return there. She was hurt by his attitude, the cold compression of his mouth when she mentioned that they would have to go back and tidy up. It was so obvious he regretted what had happened there that she changed her mind about apologising for her part in it. When she recalled his remarks about being trapped, her cheeks went hot again with humiliation. She must continue to convince him, if only by her silence on the subject, that she had no such intentions.

For the remainder of the morning and well into the afternoon they worked on the boat. Zoe, an expert on maintenance, knew exactly what to do without having to be told. She passed Reece the right tools at the right time, working quickly, with a marked intelligence, but she didn't receive any praise or expect any.

They were almost finished when he suggested a short respite for coffee. After it had been made and drunk Zoe said coolly, 'While you finish checking here, I can go back to the cottage and see to things there, if you like.'

He paused thoughtfully but didn't argue. 'I'll give you half an hour, no more.'

'That should be adequate,' she replied stiffly.

Reece glanced at her pale face with an inscrutable expression, but didn't offer to accompany her.

She soon had everything exactly as they'd found it and, to make sure, took a last look round before closing the cottage door. With difficulty she swallowed a lump in her throat. If circumstances had been different she would loved to have spent more time here. Material things had never been important to her. She would have enjoyed exploring the island, coming back to a frugal meal, cooked over the open fire, especially with Reece for company. It wouldn't have mattered about anything else.

Having forced herself to be honest, she told herself fiercely she didn't have to dwell on it. Self-knowledge could only destroy if one allowed it to, and it must surely be better to face up to things than to pretend nothing had happened. Reece Macadam didn't want her, and if for a little while she had wanted him it was something she was going to have to forget. Perhaps she would be wise to look for other employment as soon as it was possible as it wasn't going to be easy to continue working for him after this.

When she returned she was surprised to find him on the top of the cliff. 'Were you coming to help?' she asked, managing a brittle smile.

'I came to meet you,' he frowned slightly at her tone. 'Is everything all right?'

She supposed he meant the cottage and nodded. 'It's nice. I was sorry to leave.'

'We can thank God it was there,' he said dryly, 'Otherwise we could have had a bad night.'

'Could it have been any worse than the one we had?' she asked flippantly, determined to pretend she had hated being with him. The skilfulness of his love-making was something she was determined to forget.

His taut silence, the stiff rigidity of his back as he turned to go before her down the cliff path, should have made her feel triumphant, and she couldn't understand why it didn't. 'Does your writer friend want a lot for his island?' she asked rather uneasily.

'We all want a lot, these days,' Reece replied cryptically, 'but this isn't everyone's cup of tea.'

'It's beautiful, though.' On the shore, she paused staring around, her small face unconsciously wistful.

'There's nothing here for a young girl like you.'

'What sort of a girl do you think I am?' she demanded sharply, stumbling on the sand as something in his voice disconcerted her.

'That will have to keep.' His hand went out grimly to steady her until she regained her balance. 'Once I got started . . .' his glance went enigmatically over her, resting briefly on the tender curves clearly outlined as they pushed against her shrunken sweater, 'I might not be able to stop this time, and we're in a hurry.'

It was mid-evening when they reached home. Zoe, having remembered the untidy state of the galley, elected to rush below at the last minute to wash their breakfast dishes. Once they had tied up at the wharf, she wanted Reece to take her straight home. The sooner she saw her grandparents and assured them that she was safe, the better.

There was more to do than she expected and before she was finished she could tell by the motion of the boat that it was in its berth. Leaving the last few chores undone, she hastily dried her hands and went on deck. Here she stopped aghast, as a most frightening scene met her eyes.

On the quayside stood her grandfather, a veritable Goliath, his white hair and beard flowing wildly, while ranged on either side and behind him were a bunch of Macadam's men, their eyes coldly accusing.

Their prevailing silence had done nothing to warn her. They were looking at Reece, she realised, while he stood staring back at them, his own eyes hard in an entirely expressionless face.

For a brief second, as she rushed towards him, Zoe took in the equally impressive figure he made. His jeans, shrunken with sea water, clung to the powerful length of his legs, and his shirt, flung carelessly around his broad shoulders, was open to the waist. Such impressions were only fleeting, however, as her heart leapt to her throat at the danger she thought he was in. Her grandfather was advancing, looking furious enough to strike the younger man to the ground.

Panic sweeping everything else from her mind, she cried, 'Reece, watch out!' her voice, crystal clear, shattering the unnatural quiet.

'Oh, God,' she heard him mutter, 'that's all I need!'

The gasp that rose from the men was perhaps not so loud as it seemed. Nevertheless, despite her apprehension, Zoe wished she could have sunk through the deck. She knew, as they all did, that she never called Reece anything but Macadam. Suddenly, with a kind of horrified despair, she saw she had unwittingly confirmed, with a single word, the terrible suspicions written plainly on her grandfather's face.

It was like the continuation of a nightmare when Taggart began shouting at Reece, asking him what he meant by abducting his granddaughter. When Zoe desperately tried to intervene, he turned on her. 'Be quiet, young woman! Should you not be ashamed of the disgrace you've brought on my house, and all your friends here?'

Reece flung back his head, his whole body rigid, stopping Taggart with a glance. 'Will you kindly shut up!' he snapped tersely, grasping Zoe by the wrist as she again tried to interrupt. The warning pressure of his fingers forbade her to, and surprisingly, the grip of his hand conveyed a silent message that he, too, recognised a need for forbearance.

At the same time, Zoe sensed an anger rising in him which she feared might not be controlled for long. Surely her grandfather knew Reece would refuse to be intimidated?

She heard him explaining briefly, as she stood shivering by his side. 'We were caught in a storm, Taggart—you don't need me to tell you just how quickly one can blow up. We were wrecked on Sam

Colter's island. I took a nasty crack on the head, we're both lucky to be alive.'

'You might not think so before I'm through with you!' Taggart blustered, becoming angrier instead of calming down, as Zoe was praying he might. Raising a formidable finger, he pointed it straight at Reece. 'You knew the weather was unsettled, so much so that very few people were out, yet you not only went yourself but took her with you!' His finger wavered in the direction of Zoe's shrinking figure.

Her face, white as chalk, she gasped, 'No, Grandfather, that's not true! I . . .'

As she was about to confess that she had stowed away, the words were choked in her throat as Reece jerked her roughly against him. His arm went around her thin shoulders to hold her tightly.

'It's true enough, Taggart,' he lied grimly. 'As for the rest, all your other obvious and despicable suspicions, they're entirely without foundation.'

'Where did you spend the night?' Taggart, clearly outraged at being spoken to in such a fashion, appeared to lose all sense of discretion.

Zoe wanted to cry out, but found she still couldn't speak. Nor, for a moment, did Reece. Narrowly he glanced around the ring of condemning faces. If his men's expressions were anything to go by, they had already judged him and found him guilty of everything Taggart accused him of—kidnapping and seduction! Zoe heard Reece drawing a deep, hard breath while she herself went icy cold with apprehension.

CHAPTER SEVEN

At last Reece spoke, his voice so dangerously calm that the men stirred uneasily. 'I think I'd prefer to discuss this elsewhere, Taggart, if you don't mind—if you insist?'

'That would suit you fine, wouldn't it, Macadam?' Taggart raged, almost beside himself with fury. 'You stay out all night with my granddaughter and expect me to discuss it calmly another day, and at your convenience. No, sir!' his face became so red Zoe gasped with alarm, even as she dreaded what was coming. 'You've compromised my dead son's only child and, with these men as my witness, I'll have your promise of recompense right here!'

'Just what sort of compensation are you looking for?' Reece, his voice now icy with anger, stared at Taggart his eyes glittering with contempt. His whole stance, Zoe realised, would have inhibited any other man but her grandfather.

'Are you prepared to marry her?' Taggart thundered, with the men muttering and backing him up belligerently.

Almost in tears, Zoe saw that they blamed Reece entirely. He was older and so in command of every situation that they actually appeared to believe he could have avoided what had happened, if he had choosen to do so. And, terrible though it was, she found she couldn't altogether blame them, for of course they didn't know the whole truth. She felt very bitter towards them, though, that they should doubt Reece's integrity!

'Grandfather!' she cried suddenly, furiously, ignor-

113

ing Reece's arm nearly breaking her shoulder. 'You ought to be ashamed of yourself! Nothing has happened—nothing like what you appear to think. You must know it couldn't be true!'

Reece cut off her indignant protests sharply. 'Taggart,' he exclaimed lividly, 'I'll give you one last chance to come to my office or, by God, old as you are, I'll break every bone in your body! Zoe and I will be married, but not because you say so, or because of anything we've done. But I refuse to stand here wrangling in public any longer.'

Not surprisingly Taggart subsided. He was more frightened of Reece than Reece would ever be of him. Never yet had Taggart won an argument against the other man, but for the first time on losing one he didn't look altogether disgruntled.

Zoe found it difficult to speak, she was so stunned by the turn of events. Reece's terse declaration that they were to be married filled her with dismay. He was proud, but his wasn't the pride of an inflated ego. It sprang from his being able to look any man in the face. If her grandfather forced them to marry, Reece would never forgive her.

'Reece?' she whispered, staring at her grandfather in a kind of helpless fury.

'Shut up!' Reece snapped, far from lover-like.

The men faded away. Zoe blinked disbelievingly. One moment they had all been there, the next they had gone, most probably to cross wives and cold dinners. It was unlikely, because of their fundamental, unswerving loyalty to Reece, that they would mention anything of what had happened here, but things had a way of getting around.

In the office Zoe came to her senses. 'I'm not going to marry you, Macadam,' she looked at him, her teeth clenched, 'and that's five minutes overdue.'

'You can and you will,' he answered curtly. 'Listen,

Zoe,' she saw his face tighten, his eyes darken, 'I want your promise that you'll leave everything to me.'

'I hope I have a choice!' she heard her grandfather panting up the stairs behind them.

'No,' said Reece.

'I'll tell you this,' she cried, but so only he could hear. 'I'll never allow you to sacrifice everything by marrying me!'

A mocking grin split his face at that and she wanted to ask what was so funny.

There followed a scene almost as confusing to Zoe as the one which had taken place on the yacht. Instead of continuing to bluster, Taggart lapsed into sullen utterances, with Reece terse to the point of rudeness. The final outcome was clear enough, though, even to Zoe's shocked, incredulous mind. Reece and she would be married—and very quickly. She, apparently, was to have no say in the matter. Even a date for the wedding was set, Reece deciding it should be in less than a month's time.

When Taggart was dispatched in a taxi, with a promise from Reece that he and Zoe would follow in a few minutes, Zoe lifted her head to meet Reece's hooded eyes. She had listened silently, having been grimly ordered by Reece to be quiet each time she had attempted to interrupt the bitter exchange of words between the two men. Now, trembling from head to foot, she swallowed convulsively, trying to rid herself of a choking sensation of fear. A fear which still edged her voice when she did manage to speak.

'Reece—about getting married. You can't be serious?'

'No?' He went to pour them each a drink, telling her abruptly to drink hers up because she looked as if she needed it.

'Are you surprised?' she asked angrily, obeying him because she did feel dreadfully in need of something.

'Surely you don't believe that was a lot of idle chatter?' he jeered, without sympathy.

She took a quicker drink and some went up her nose, bringing tears to her eyes. 'I realise Grandfather had to be pacified.'

'What a naïve little mind you have!'

'I'm trying to think,' she cried, hating both him and her grandfather.

'Then keep on trying,' he taunted. 'You'll soon get the hang of it—and used to the idea of being married. Most women seem to like it until the novelty wears off.'

Ignoring his sarcasm, she protested fiercely, 'But I can't marry you!'

'Well, you aren't marrying anyone else.' Picking up some of the pile of unopened mail on his desk, he flipped through it indifferently and laid it down again. 'You'll just have to forget the other men in your life, I'm afraid.'

Didn't he know how she felt? All these other men he mentioned, where were they? She never saw anyone but him. Lately she had had a dream, but it had been ruined this weekend, first by Reece, now her grandfather. Dear God, didn't he understand?

'Reece . . .' the brandy she had swallowed gave her courage, 'the whole thing's ridiculous, don't pretend you think it isn't. What happened out there was like a scene from a Shakespeare play. No one could possibly take it seriously!'

'You think not?' His brows rose sardonically, 'You saw the faces of the men, especially when you called me Reece.'

She flushed but stubbornly shook her head. 'If my grandfather hadn't been there they wouldn't have given that, or our being away together a second thought.'

'How do you know?' he growled, swallowing his own

drink in one go and getting rid of the glass. Putting his hands on the arms of the chair where she sat frozen, he leant over her. 'Look at me, Zoe. Have we ever been away like this before? You're forgetting I don't run a huge, impersonal concern. This is a family business. These men have looked after you, protected you since you were a small child.'

'But they're blaming you for something which never happened!'

'It might easily have done.' He didn't spare her, not even when her cheeks were scarlet. 'Don't you see, the damage has been done and it's up to me to put things right.'

'And you really think, by marrying me, you can do that?' Her anguished green eyes begged for understanding. 'Don't you realise that a forced marriage would be much worse than a little gossip and speculation? That might soon be forgotten, but if we marry people won't ever forget.'

Reece's jaw went tight. 'Nonsense,' he replied crisply. 'That kind of gossip becomes boring in time. As soon as everyone sees we're happily married they'll soon forget. Besides, few people will really believe I didn't know what I was doing.'

'But you didn't, did you?' Her eyes darkened with pain. 'Why didn't you let me tell them I'd stowed away?'

'Because it's irrelevant, and I prefer to take the blame, if we must use the word, on my own shoulders. They're broad enough,' he added dryly. 'This way, your friends in the yard might feel sorry for you, but that's all.'

'You don't love me,' Zoe said starkly. This, to her, although she wouldn't confess it, seemed the most important reason why they should not marry. 'You— you're fond of Ursula Findlay. You might have been happier with someone like her.'

'I might have,' he agreed coolly.

That he didn't deny it hurt like physical pain. 'You were friends with her a long time.'

'Yes,' he said, 'but I'm sure she'll understand.'

What sort of answer was that? Zoe felt torn to shreds by the torment of not knowing. If he was determined to carry out this farce to the bitter end, why didn't he go the whole way, take her in his arms and at least pretend he had some affection for her? Wouldn't it be a whole lot better than sowing doubts in her mind about Ursula Findlay?

'You said you didn't want to be trapped,' she accused, remembering.

Impatiently he retorted, 'We both said a lot of things last night, Zoe, which would be better forgotten. I suggest we put such an unfortunate episode from us and start afresh.'

'You're asking the impossible!' she gasped.

'Nothing's impossible,' he taunted, 'but go on suffering if you must. I've noticed some people get a great deal of pleasure out of torturing themselves.' Lifting a hand from the arm of her chair, he tilted her chin with it to study her pale, tired face. 'One thing is certain, you aren't going to feel any better until you get home and get some rest, so come on.'

As he let go of her trembling chin, straightening away from her without touching her again, Zoe knew instinctively that he would rather do anything than give her a comforting hug. He probably didn't trust himself not to murder her!

Bleakly, as she rose to her feet, she asked, 'What happens in the morning?'

Curtly he held the office door open for her. 'You come in and carry on as usual, or, should I say, as if nothing unusual had happened.' Mockingly he added, 'I have no doubt, by then, you'll have recovered your temper, as well as everything else.'

At her grandparents' house he dropped her off with a brief goodnight, refusing to linger. To Zoe's surprise she found her grandmother alone. She had hot soup waiting and a pot of freshly made tea. Zoe didn't feel she could eat anything, but rather than disappoint Janet, who had obviously gone to a lot of trouble, she tackled the soup while Janet poured two cups of tea.

Her grandmother sat down opposite at the kitchen table, stirring a spoonful of sugar into hers thoughtfully. 'Your grandfather's gone to bed,' she said. 'He's feeling tired and a bit ashamed of himself.'

'So he should be,' Zoe replied stiffly.

'I know,' Janet sighed softly, 'but when you didn't return we got terribly worried. By this morning your grandfather was nearly beside himself, and I'm afraid Mr Macadam's message didn't help much. Oh, it was good to know you were safe, but Mr Macadam made it sound as if there'd been little to prevent you from getting back if you'd tried.'

'But you've no idea what it was like!' Zoe protested. 'The storm was dreadful!'

'Well, I believe we must have missed the worst of it,' Janet said gently, as Zoe paused. 'I was talking to Bill McGregor a few minutes ago and he said it was bad farther out. But your grandfather was in a rare state by this evening, child.'

'You can say that again!' Zoe exclaimed, in no mood to be pacified. 'Oh, Gran, you should have seen him! In front of all the men he practically forced Reece to promise to marry me!'

Janet's face was almost as pale as her grandaughter's. 'So he tells me,' she whispered. 'However,' she went on more firmly, 'the men are good and loyal. No more will be heard of it. Your grandfather has relented, he won't force anyone to do anything. He will be seeing Mr Macadam tomorrow and apologise for his hastiness. There won't be any wedding.'

Zoe got up early to go to the office and, as she came downstairs, she saw a note lying on the floor beside the front door. It was from Reece, requesting her to stay at home as he would be away all day. He would see her in the morning. It was signed, yours, as ever, Reece Macadam.

He must have left it hours ago, because she had been awake for ages and heard no sound. Where had he gone? she wondered. She read the note again while drinking a cup of tea and nibbling halfheartedly at a slice of toast. She still felt too worried to enjoy eating anything.

Her grandfather had come to her room last night and had been full of remorse. He swore he had never intended challenging Reece as he had done. He had lost his temper and was sorry. He would see Reece as soon as he could in the morning and put things right. He confirmed what he had said to Janet about there being no need for a wedding. If Zoe saw Reece, he said, before he did, she could tell him so.

How could she tell Reece if she didn't know where to find him? Cold with unhappiness and tension, she pondered. She had passed a terrible night, despite her grandfather's reassurances that all would be well, and she felt dreadful. It was almost too much of an effort to think.

Eventually she left Reece's note for Taggart to read. It would save him making an unnecessary journey to the yard. To the bottom of it she added a brief message of her own, that she'd decided to go in anyway, to deal with the backlog of correspondence, but wouldn't be long. Secretly she nursed a vague hope that Reece might have changed his mind about going away and be there, after all. The news she had for him was burning her up, she didn't know if it would keep until tomorrow.

He wasn't at the office. His room was empty and

silent. Zoe looked at his chair and sat down in it briefly with tears in her eyes. The men behaved exactly as Reece said they would. They spoke to her as though nothing unusual had happened. Reece's yacht bobbed gently in its berth in the pale morning sunshine, she found it difficult to even glance at it. Ian returned from his long weekend surprised to find Reece absent. Zoe merely said he was out for the day, she didn't know where, but Ian didn't ask any questions. After dealing with the mail, as far as she could, she left before he grew curious.

She spent the rest of the day wandering aimlessly. Hopefully she rang Reece's house during the afternoon, but received no answer and, although she walked the length of the town several times, she didn't bump into him anywhere.

After another restless night, Zoe rose early again and hurried to the boatyard. Reece was there, as he had said he would be but for a few moments she had difficulty in believing it. Her heart raced and the aching emptiness inside her became an actual pain.

'Reece!' she exclaimed breathlessly. Please let him be kind to me, she prayed.

'Zoe!' He glanced up from his desk with familiar disapproval. 'Must you rush around like a schoolgirl? I would rather my future wife conducted herself with a little more dignity.'

'Your future—what?' Ian asked behind her.

'You heard,' said Reece, seeming pleased at Ian's angry dismay, if nothing else. Ignoring the silent, frantic message Zoe was trying to convey, he enlightened Ian smoothly, 'It happened over the weekend. Now, if you'll excuse us, I'd like a private word with my fiancée. And a chance to kiss her good-morning,' he added, as the door closed.

'Have you no sense!' Zoe snapped, as Ian's footsteps receded. Agitated beyond reason, she glared at Reece.

'I tried to find you all yesterday to tell you grand-father's relented. You don't have to marry me any more. He lost his temper.'

For an answer, if it was one, Reece rose, jerking her to him, and a peculiar sensation of alarmed confusion widened her eyes. Time stood still as his arms tight-ened and his mouth touched her own. For the first few moments the pressure he exerted was light and warm. Then he pressed her closer and his mouth seemed to burn her like a brand, as if he was determined to stamp his ownership once and for all. Her head spinning, she was aware of his rising desire which her shameless body seemed bent on satisfying. Her arms had some-how found their way round his neck and she was clinging to him.

With a strangled cry she pulled herself free, groping, like a young animal suddenly blinded, towards the window and the light. She turned to face him with the advantage of a few moments' respite. Her voice was cool, she had control of herself again.

'Didn't you hear what I said?' she asked.

'My hearing, I suppose, is average,' he taunted. 'At least, I hope so, since you've chosen to remove yourself to such a distance.'

Why had she this feeling he was playing for time? 'You're free,' she repeated. 'My grandfather's changed his mind.'

'But I haven't changed mine,' Reece jeered, anger smouldering softly in his eyes. 'We're engaged and that's that! If you think I'm turning my life upside down a second time, you're mistaken.'

'Oh, don't be so silly!' Zoe was so aggravated she almost stamped her small foot. 'It concerns me as well as you. It's not just what you like! Besides . . .' she snatched desperately at the first thing to cross her mind to support her argument, 'Besides, you don't love me.'

'So we're back to that, are we?' he mocked. 'Love,

my child, is wasted energy. It simply makes me ache in the most inconvenient places.'

'You've been—you are in love?' she faltered, not willing to believe it.

'For some time,' his face went cynically grim, 'but the lady doesn't love me. I've tried about everything and nothing works, so I've decided to get married without it.'

His change of mood caught her by surprise and the flush of anger faded from her cheeks. Reece didn't know she loved him. He wouldn't think he was doing her any real harm by marrying her, but how could she possibly marry him, especially now that she knew he loved someone else? Lord, what a mix-up!

'We won't do so badly, Zoe,' he coaxed softly, crossing to her and taking hold of her with a slight grin. 'You're beautiful, I'm handsome . . .'

She jerked away from him again—not because she wanted to but because she couldn't trust herself not to respond to the gentler note in his voice. He couldn't be too much in love with another woman if he could tease her like this, could he? All the same, the temptation to fall weakly into his arms was not to be considered.

'Please, Reece,' her eyes unconsciously pleaded with him, 'we aren't engaged any more.'

'My darling,' he jeered, his voice low and taunting, 'we are. It's going to be in all the papers this morning. Why do you think I was in Edinburgh yesterday?'

'So that's where you were?'

'After I'd seen the minister and fixed a date for our wedding here. Exactly a month from last Monday.'

Zoe stared at him incredulously. 'Now I know you're mad! And why this obsession with a month?' She felt near hysterics. 'Why not tomorrow or next year!'

Reece didn't lose his temper, as hers rose, as normally he might. 'Wait and see,' was all he said.

A net was closing in on her. She couldn't understand his attitude. He was ignoring every protest she made. 'If only I'd seen you yesterday!' she groaned, 'Why did you go to Edinburgh? You didn't have to. If you felt it was necessary, you could have contacted the newspapers about our engagement over the phone.'

'I went to see my parents.'

'Your—parents?'

'I do have some, you know,' he said quietly, 'same as our children are going to have. A father and mother.'

Her heart lurched. How cruel could you get? As things were between them, children wouldn't be possible. 'Why did you see them?' she asked. 'Was it merely that you were there—coincidence?'

'No coincidence,' he shook his head. 'I went to tell them personally about our engagement before putting the notice in the papers. It was the right thing to do.'

When had that ever worried him? Zoe glared at him suspiciously, her nerves tense. He was too suave. One would think he was planning a campaign! 'And?' she prompted woodenly, sure there was more to come.

There was. 'They're coming here tomorrow to meet you. It's all arranged. They're looking forward to it.'

She was sure! 'Well, how nice for—for somebody.' Another time she might have been ashamed of the carping note in her voice but, right now, she didn't care. 'I thought you weren't friends?'

'We're not, but on occasions like this one must observe the priorities.'

'Hypocrite!' she hissed.

'I always appreciate your frank opinion,' Reece smiled unperturbed, magnificently impregnable, breathtakingly masculine in black sweater and pants. 'Only I hope it won't always be as frank.'

Was he warning her, threatening? She didn't care

for the glint in his eyes. 'My grandfather will be arriving at any minute,' she remembered desperately, her mind swinging off at a tangent, drunkenly.

'No,' Reece had yet another move worked out beforehand, too quick for her, 'I sent word, forbidding him to come. I'm meeting him at his house instead— I'm on my way there now, to see both him and your grandmother. While you occupy yourself here,' he added, 'there's plenty to do.'

Zoe was overcome by panic. 'I can't stay here! I have to go with you. If I don't you'll talk them into seeing things your way . . .'

'If you attempt to come with me I'll tie you in that chair,' he flicked a hand at it, 'and lock the door. I'll also gag you and block the keyhole, in case our Mr Graham gets curious.'

'You can't!' Suddenly she had a horrible feeling he could. 'Oh, Reece,' she cried, 'please be sensible. We can't get married!'

Suddenly he had her by the shoulders and she didn't doubt again that he was serious. 'Listen to me, Zoe Kerr,' he said grimly, 'you got me into this and if you think you're going to avoid going through with it then you're mistaken. I don't intend to be made to look a fool twice. Besides, as I think I've already mentioned, I could do with a convenient wife.'

A strange emotion rose inside her, nothing she could immediately identify, a mixture of resentment and surrender, rolled into one. His fingers dug into her shoulders and his face was dark and taut. Her heart trembled frighteningly, as the chains which bound her to him seemed to tighten. 'I think I'm the one who's trapped,' she exclaimed, with bitter emphasis.

Reece merely shrugged and let go of her.

'Will—will your parents be staying long?' she asked dully, watching him prepare to leave.

'Probably a week. Then no more until the wedding.'

'A—a week!' Zoe wished she could stop stammering. 'Where will they stay? At your house?'

'My dear mother,' Reece drawled, 'wouldn't be caught dead in it. Not now. No, she booked in immediately at her favourite hotel. We're all dining together tomorrow evening.'

'All?' Zoe swallowed distractedly. 'Who's all, for heaven's sake?'

He looked back over his shoulder as he went out. 'Who do you think? The two of us, two of them and your grandparents.'

It was really incredible, Zoe thought unhappily, not for the first time, what Reece Macadam achieved when he set his mind to it. He should have been a P.R. man. Not only had he managed to convince Taggart that his untimely intervention had merely precipitated plans Reece had already made to marry Zoe, he had also persuaded both her grandparents that it was what Zoe wanted herself. On top of this he had talked them into having dinner with his parents, with presumably little effort. Zoe could see they were pleased that everything was settled and, without hurting them, there seemed nothing she could do but give in gracefully. That, she decided, she would do for the moment, while never allowing herself to believe the marriage would ever take place.

Reece's parents rang his office to say they had arrived and later in the day Reece picked up Zoe and her grandparents and drove them to the hotel for dinner. Zoe wore a long green dress for the occasion, a pretty dress with a low, rounded neckline which complemented her soft green eyes and pale gold hair. Her grandparents already knew Reece's mother, although they hadn't seen her since she had married, but neither of them had met his father. When Zoe, unable to contain her curiosity, had asked her grandmother what Mrs Macadam was like, Janet had replied evasively that from what she could remember she was very nice.

As they entered the hotel Zoe felt quite proud of her grandparents. Janet wore blue, and with her silver hair softly waved was, in her seventies, still a very pretty woman. And Taggart, dignified and quietly dressed in one of his fine grey churchgoing suits, was still a fine figure of a man. If there was a coolness between him and Reece it wasn't noticeable, and Zoe was relieved. She didn't feel like taking sides. She considered both men partly to blame for what had happened. The initial fault had been hers for stowing away, and her grandfather had been too hasty, but she was still convinced that if Reece had gone about things in a different way the subsequent turn of events could have been avoided. In rushing off to Edinburgh and publicly announcing their engagement, he appeared to have acted impulsively. This puzzled Zoe as he wasn't impulsive by nature. Usually he was so clear-sighted he had no need to be.

The Macadams were waiting in one of the lounges. Reece put his arm round Zoe's waist, drawing her towards them. She caught her breath as she met his father. He bore little resemblance to his son apart from his eyes, where there was a marked similarity. It gave her a peculiar feeling to think that two men possessed the same penetrating gaze. His mother was elegant and smart, very sure of herself, a trait Zoe immediately recognised in Reece.

Everyone was shaking hands and Reece's mother was remembering Janet had taught her at school and there appeared to be a lot of good will around. Everyone talked. No one noticed Zoe was quiet. She wasn't sure what to make of Reece's parents. They didn't scare her, but they obviously came from a different world. Surprisingly Janet and Taggart were more at home with them than she was. Her grandmother, especially, always took a great interest in everything and could talk well on many subjects which made good dinner table conversation.

Zoe felt Reece's mocking eyes on her frequently and was slightly indignant. No one was asking her anything, so was it her fault if she didn't seem to be joining in? She sat beside Reece, at his right hand, and, between courses, he often availed himself of her left hand, his fingers caressing her brand new ring.

She thought he was touching it absently until he murmured in her ear, 'I hope it always reminds you that you belong to me.'

Zoe shivered, and knew he felt the tremor which shook her, because he smiled with a cool satisfaction.

'Are you staying long?' Janet was asking the Macadams.

'A few days, no longer,' Fiona replied. 'I want to look up a few old friends, especially the Findlays. Ursula, you know, sometimes stays with me in Edinburgh. A dear girl.' She glanced at Reece and Zoe fancied her eyes were slightly reproachful.

Zoe felt cold suddenly as she stared at her glass of wine. What's the matter with me? she thought, but she knew. She hadn't been aware that Ursula Findlay knew Reece's people so well. In fact she hadn't realised they were even acquainted. The feeling which consumed her was very like jealousy, but she refused to believe it.

'You must come and see us before you go. We must arrange a time?' Janet smiled.

'Of course,' Fiona agreed politely. Then, less enthusiastically, 'I suppose there'll be the wedding to discuss. I expect, though, it will be quiet.'

The actual wedding hadn't been mentioned yet. Zoe noticed that Janet appeared rather at a loss.

Before she could speak, Reece intervened. 'That will be entirely up to Zoe. Whatever she wants.'

'When my younger son married, Karen's parents,

Sir Malcolm and Lady Lauder, gave their daughter a beautiful wedding.'

'Yes, Mother,' Reece agreed dryly, 'but neither Zoe or I want anything like that. We might not be able to afford the glitter, but I'm sure we have something much more endurable and worthwhile.'

Fiona frowned but recovered quickly. She always would, Zoe thought, half admiring, half despairing. Fiona pointedly ignored Reece, addressing herself again to Janet. 'Our other son runs the family business now. He's been a great comfort since Reece deserted.'

Janet nodded but said nothing, while Reece's brows rose sardonically, without obvious remorse. A little later the party broke up.

Before they left, Fiona insisted Zoe join her for coffee next morning. 'Reece can spare you, so you have no excuse,' she overruled, as Zoe began to protest. 'We must have a little chat and get to know each other.'

'Certainly,' Reece drawled dryly.

Reece ran the Kerrs home, but held Zoe back to say goodnight. 'Enjoy yourself?' he asked lightly.

'It was much easier than I thought it might be,' she answered frankly. 'I don't know if your mother and I will ever be friends, but I think I could like her.'

'It's not important,' he shrugged, and she saw he meant it.

'You really have cut yourself off from your family,' she said wonderingly.

'We lead different lives.'

Then why had he gone to all the trouble of bringing them here? And everyone would soon realise they were here. If he had considered it so necessary that they should meet his bride-to-be, perhaps they were more important to him than he realised?

'What if your mother should discover the truth?' she asked, doubtful if she could bear it.

'By the truth, I presume you mean what happened on Monday evening?'

'Yes.'

'She isn't likely to. If she did hear anything it would only be a rumour, and I think she would tackle me first.'

Zoe could tell by his tone that he was irritated that she couldn't just forget all about it. How like a man! How could she forget about something like that? Unhappily she persisted. 'But if she asked me, I should have to tell her the truth.'

'Refer her to me,' he retorted indifferently. 'My skin's thick enough, I'm not sure yours is.'

'I couldn't put her off just like that!' Zoe protested, wishing she could.

'Oh, God!' he muttered, hitting a tight fist on the steering wheel. 'Heaven preserve me from an honest woman! But if the contingency does arise, and I don't believe it will, make very sure you know the whole truth before you begin.'

'Could you explain that, please?' Her smooth brow wrinkled.

'Another time,' Reece put her off, taunting enigmatically. 'If I could be sure of getting more than just a goodnight kiss I might be willing to go to a lot more trouble.'

'You aren't even getting that!' she replied tartly, turning to leave him.

'Never challenge a man,' he mocked, his dark face hardening, 'especially your future husband.'

'Don't be so sure,' she snapped back.

'I'd like to make very sure.' He drew her back against him ruthlessly, taking his kiss in such a way as to leave her gasping. His eyes went over her trembling, weakening figure intimately and tauntingly, his meaning very clear. 'If a car was constructed differently, and the consequences were less risky, I would make you eat those words, Zoe Kerr!'

CHAPTER EIGHT

REECE approved the softly styled skirt and silky blouse she wore to have coffee with his mother, the slenderness of her legs and narrow feet encased in fragile, strapped high-heeled sandals.

'You look very nice, Zoe,' he said, with a slightly wicked grin. 'It makes a nice change from jeans.' Before she quite realised what he was doing, his hand went out to release the top few buttons of the blouse. 'That's better,' he murmured, his eyes lingering on the white skin of her throat appreciatively. 'Not so constricted-looking.'

Feeling scorched by the touch of his fingers, Zoe flinched. There was nothing in his behaviour she could really take exception to but she distrusted the deepening blue of his glance, his drawling tones. 'I'm not sure your mother will approve,' she retorted, her pulses racing. Where had he learnt to be so deft?

'My father's spending the morning with me, so you'll be entirely at her mercy,' Reece grinned, again with a little amusement as she stared at him glumly, a moment before he dropped her off at the hotel. It surprised her that he considered her up to it.

Mrs Macadam was waiting, obviously feeling up to anything. As she and Zoe surveyed each other warily over coffee cups, she smiled sweetly. 'You and Reece might suit each other, of course. Years ago I faced up to the fact that he might marry a girl like you, but I'll admit I'm disappointed.'

Zoe admired Mrs Macadam's frankness if nothing else. 'Had you hopes in another direction?' she asked innocently.

'I had thought of Ursula Findlay,' Mrs Macadam broke a sugary biscuit with an impatient sigh, as if it should all have been so simple. 'I've known her parents all my life. Reece knew Ursula even before he came here, but I always told her if she wanted to catch him she should show more interest in boats and such things.'

What were—such things? 'Miss Findlay doesn't care for getting wet and dirty.'

'No, but she likes Reece,' Mrs Macadam frowned, 'and I thought Reece was in love with her. I don't know what went wrong, but I suspect it had something to do with his business. He doesn't have enough time to devote to her and he'll never be a millionaire.'

'Is being a millionaire important?' Zoe asked in astonishment.

'To a girl like Ursula it is,' Mrs Macadam nodded admiringly.

Zoe thought of well-worn clichés she might have quoted, but stirred her coffee instead.

'Where will you live when you're married?' Mrs Macadam asked next, as if they had merely been discussing the weather. 'In that monstrosity of my late brother's on the hill, I suppose?'

'Yes.' Zoe forgot all about her coffee and looked up sharply, feeling oddly defensive. 'I think it's very nice.'

'That was something else against Ursula,' Mrs Macadam said. 'She hates it, always has. Not that I can blame her. If I were you, my dear child, I should insist on having the whole place done out from top to bottom before I set foot inside it.'

Zoe was secretly relieved when the Macadams returned to Edinburgh, but did her best to show some enthusiasm when they promised to come back for the wedding. The worst part of their visit had been when Mrs Macadam brought Ursula to the office one morning and the girl had flirted with Reece until Zoe had felt near to tears.

Why was Reece so sure Ursula didn't love him? She certainly made no pretence of being pleased that he was marrying another girl. Despairingly she watched them laughing together, Reece's dark head bent over Ursula's even darker one. What did all these women see in him? she wondered, wishing she didn't know. Carol Vintis had rung earlier, asking if it was true, what she'd just heard about Zoe and Reece being engaged? The other girl had been frankly dismayed when Zoe had reluctantly confirmed it.

'I was falling in love with him myself,' she'd groaned. 'Just my luck!'

Zoe didn't know why she couldn't find the courage to tell Ursula and Carol, and all his other lady friends, that she had no intention of marrying him. It should have been easy, so why allow a certain glint in his eye, each time she was brooding on the subject, to deter her? It was as if he read her thoughts and was daring her to do it. She felt a terrible coward that she was looking for a foolproof excuse, and she looked in vain. Until the day Ian Graham provided her with one.

Reece was out. Ian strolled into her office and closed the door. 'All alone, darling?' he smiled.

Giving him a wry glance, Zoe didn't reply. Her fine feathery eyebrows merely rose a fraction.

'Ask a silly question,' he shrugged.

'Exactly.'

He laughed, sitting on the edge of her desk. 'You sound so prim when you say that.'

Something tightened in her cautiously. 'And you sound as though you don't believe it's true.'

His eyes narrowed thoughtfully as he fiddled idly with one of her pens. 'I've been hearing things, darling.'

'What?' she enquired slowly, horrified to feel her cheeks burning hot.

'Oh,' he said softly, 'just this and that.'

'Ian!' she exclaimed, her heart thumping with a strange apprehension, 'I hate people who beat about the bush, hiding behind stupid innuendoes. Just what have you been hearing?'

Again he paused. 'Just something which makes me want to know more. Such as why you and Reece weren't in the office all day Monday, a week last Monday, that is, and why he was in Edinburgh the next day with a bandage round his head.'

Zoe stared at him, all her colour fading. Reece had been hurt, but he had insisted he wasn't. He'd said it had only been a light blow, even though it had knocked him out. Anxiously she asked Ian, 'Did you say his head was bandaged?'

'Surprised, sweetie?' Ian's sceptical glance challenged her to say yes.

'No.' Bewildered, she shook her head. 'But you'd better ask him . . .'

'Ah!' Ian pounced triumphantly. 'So you do know! I heard a rumour that there's been some strange goings-on.' He bent nearer, smiling persuasively. 'Come on, darling, spill the beans. I'm eaten up with curiosity. Reece with a sore head, surprise engagements and everyone clamming up as if they were guarding a state secret. When I asked down there,' he threw a derisive hand in the direction of the yard, 'all I got was wooden silence.'

'What did you expect?' Zoe muttered indistinctly, relieved beyond measure when the telephone rang in Ian's office and he had to go. He wouldn't get anything out of the men, but she was still uneasy.

Reece ran her home when he returned, but it wasn't until they were having dinner together later in the evening that she mentioned Ian.

'I think he knows something.'

Reece, ruggedly handsome in a dark blue suit and lighter, toning shirt, glanced at her quizzically, not obviously disturbed. 'What makes you think so?'

'He asked me about it today,' Zoe stammered, wondering indignantly why he had to treat her like a child who needed humouring. 'He appears to have got hold of some sort of story. He knows, apparently, that we were both away somewhere together, a week last Monday and—and you were seen in Edinburgh with a—with your head bandaged.'

'Our friend Ian's missed his true vocation,' Reece drawled. 'Had he not been so keen on boats, he might have made a good sleuth.'

'It isn't snooping, surely, just to see someone?'

'Not until you begin trying to ferret more out, the way Graham's doing. However, there's nothing to worry about. If he did manage to uncover everything, which is unlikely, he's going to be very disappointed.'

Zoe wasn't so sure, but she had more important things on her mind. 'I knew about Edinburgh, of course, but not the bandage!' She stared at him accusingly, her eyes too bright. 'Where did that come from—or go to, for that matter?'

Reece viewed her tears curiously but merely said, 'I woke that morning with a headache no aspirin could cure, so I popped in to see my doctor before leaving for Edinburgh. He wanted me to go for an X-ray, because of the bump I'd had, but I didn't have time. He gave me a shot and insisted on a bandage, which I must admit made me feel better.'

'I didn't see it.'

'No,' he sounded bored. 'When I returned that evening, I went to the office to check up. It was late and I'd had a long day and suddenly having my head bandaged irritated me. I was actually busy taking the thing off when Donald came in and caught me.'

'You must have been mad!' Zoe exclaimed.

'Donald thought so, too.'

'Did you have an X-ray?'

'No.'

'Oh!' Zoe glared at him, her green eyes pools of angry frustration. 'Obviously that blow on the head didn't knock any sense into you!'

'You can say that again,' he taunted. 'I haven't been the same since.'

'As good a reason as any why we shouldn't marry,' she said quickly. 'I told you you didn't know what you were doing. In fact, I'm not going to marry you!' she added, mistakenly brash because of his thoughtful expression.

In an instant his face was cold with self-derision. 'Sometimes I really believe I do need my head examined for allowing you to torment me as you do. If I do need a wife,' he snapped, 'you're certainly not ideal for the position, yet come hell or high water I'm determined to marry you.'

'You can't drag me to the altar!' She was as determined to defy him.

'There are more ways than one of doing that,' he retorted, his glance running over her deliberately, and in such a fashion as to turn her cheeks a fiery red.

'Opportunity is a fine thing,' she choked. 'I'm quite capable of shouting for help.'

'Do you think you would be rescued as quickly now?' Reece jeered. 'When you became my fiancée you passed into my keeping. You became my property, if you like. No one would dare interfere.'

'I—I'd scream the place down if you so much as laid a finger on me!' Her lovely green eyes glared defiance.

'You wouldn't scream long, my darling.'

He stood up abruptly and called for the bill. When he had received it, and paid it, they left.

'We didn't have coffee,' Zoe complained, outside.

'Did we want any?' he asked sardonically, almost thrusting her into the passenger seat of his car.

Driving a little way out of the town, he stopped but didn't park. Turning sideways, he glanced at her mutinous face steadily. 'Now that we've got the main issue settled, can we go somewhere and discuss our honeymoon? I thought of going to the house and taking a look at that at the same time. You might want something changed, although we'll have to leave any major changes until after the wedding.'

'No, thank you,' she replied stonily.

'Zoe,' he exclaimed, 'you aren't by any chance sulking?'

'No.' She squirmed as he regarded her suspiciously, wondering how she could bear to contemplate a future lived under his eagle and overbearing eye. Had he loved her she might have been keener to have another look at his house, but, as things were, she had no desire to be alone there with him. In such an intimate setting she might all too easily betray her own feelings.

'You're sure?' he asked.

Was he talking about the house or her moods? She slanted him a curious glance before turning away in confusion. His eyes were on her, a certain expression in them caused her emotions to jumble crazily, until she was incapable of sorting them out. As if magnetically controlled her gaze returned to him, caught in the smouldering glow of his, and for one shattering moment she was removed from the world of reality. His eyes, gleaming blue, seemed to catch her up in something much stronger than herself.

'The house is lovely,' she said huskily. 'I don't think I'll ever want to alter it. I've seen your bedroom and I don't suppose it's much different from what mine will be.' As his mouth tightened, she rushed on, trying to please him, 'I've cooked meals in the kitchen, there's nothing wrong with that. I haven't been in the lounge, but I expect you own a comfy chair or two. What more could a girl want?'

'Hmm,' his mouth relaxed a little as he considered her closely, 'I'm not sure I'll be as easily satisfied.'

'One day,' Zoe warned him innocently, 'I might demand more.'

'So might I,' he said, so smoothly her cheeks went pink. 'So that just leaves our honeymoon.'

'H—honeymoon?' she stammered, feeling feverish.

'Newly married people often have one,' Reece drawled, a familiar glint returning to his eyes.

'Yes, well——' Zoe licked dry lips, a process he followed too closely for comfort. Swallowing, she tried again. 'It's rather different in our case, isn't it?'

'Why should it be?' His mocking glance dared her to pursue the matter. 'I thought of taking you to Mexico. I still have to see that chap who wouldn't deal with Ian about the boat contract.'

Zoe frowned, feeling suddenly bleak. Was this Reece's way of letting her know he considered their marriage merely a business proposition? A tactful, silent declaration that he wouldn't make demands she wasn't prepared to meet. Or had he realised she would refuse to meet them and intended using this man in Mexico as a means of escaping a reluctant wife?

'You mean to combine business with pleasure?' she noted coolly, yet was annoyed with herself for mentioning the last word.

'Is there to be any pleasure, Zoe?' Reece asked meaningfully. 'You've shown no signs of experiencing any since becoming engaged to me.'

'The circumstances have hardly been conducive to it, have they?' she asked, with a sort of bitter defiance. 'How can I possibly forget how it all happened?'

'I can't tell you how to do that, I'm afraid,' he replied, so smoothly she wasn't aware of his anger until too late. 'But if you let a sore fester it will only get worse.'

'Don't preach to me!' she exclaimed.

'You asked my opinion, and if I wasn't on the highway I might have expressed it better without words.'

At the unmistakable threat in his voice, she flinched unhappily, while her heart raced. In a way he was right. What he didn't realise was that she loved him. How was she to forget that?

She knew better than to ask as he suddenly revved the engine and drove on impatiently. Making a brief detour to avoid returning through the town, he pulled up, out of sight, a little way past her grandparents' house.

'Well?' Turning to her, he placed his left hand on the back of her seat. 'How about the honeymoon? You've had time to think.'

'Was that what I was supposed to be doing?' she edged from the fingers lightly exploring her nape, 'I thought it was settled—a working one.'

He smiled thinly but didn't contradict her. 'Well?'

'I don't mind what we do,' she sighed, wishing he would just go ahead with whatever he chose and not talk about it any more. 'I wouldn't mind if we stayed at home, Reece.'

'Neither would I,' he said shortly, 'had things been different, Zoe. As it is, I think you need time.'

The implication was so clear she flushed and exclaimed impulsively, 'Ours can't be a normal marriage. You don't love me.'

'Couples can have normal marriages without love.'

'I don't believe it!'

'Nor can I believe you're so incredibly naïve,' he reprimanded dryly. 'Or are you tempting me to prove it?'

'No, I am not!' Zoë hated the slight tremor in her voice which took away some of the emphasis.

She must have given the impression of greater resolution than she thought. His eyes glinted as he leaned nearer. 'Such conviction,' he taunted, 'could do with a little shaking.'

Without giving her a chance to move, his mouth met hers, crushing off her protests just as she got started. Her heart began beating fast again and her thoughts became anything but clear. As his arms drew her closer and tightened, it was all too easy to succumb. With a single movement he pinned her head against him, achieving his objective by raking his fingers through her hair.

When he took his mouth from hers, her gaze clung to him as a sob shuddered through her. She stared up at him, her eyes fixed on the smouldering darkness of his, wishing she could read his expression. There was warmth in his gaze, but what did that tell her? She didn't have to wait long for an answer. As he resumed his assault on her quivering lips, she suddenly flinched. He was taking, not giving. He wasn't filling her with an assurance that everything would be all right. He was flooding her with fear, giving her more than a hint of what he was capable of if she drove him to anger.

A low moan escaped her as his mouth harshly parted hers, burning the soft inner flesh, probing until she couldn't find breath, until her senses swam and were consumed as a blaze of fire took over. Reece's hand slid to her breast, fanning the fire still further. Rendered almost mindless because of it, she clung to him, her arms finding their way round his neck, clutching him frantically, as if determined to make him a part of her.

When he pushed her away his breathing was hoarse, his heavy lids lowered, but, when he raised them, his eyes were still curiously expressionless. 'Doesn't that prove something of what's possible without love?' he murmured sardonically.

For an answer, because she was incapable of giving a sensible one, Zoe wrenched out of the car and ran from him, back down the road towards her home. In a few seconds his headlights followed her, staying behind her until she was safely inside. Then she heard his goodnight toot as he roared off.

Reece didn't ask her about their honeymoon, or to visit his house again. It was as though he was even more reluctant than she was, now, that they should be alone together there. Right up to the eve of their wedding she insisted that she didn't want to marry him, but he continued to ignore her protests.

She actually had few opportunities of speaking to him by himself during the two weeks leading up to the wedding. He was working late, and she was busy herself with preparations which began mounting amazingly. It wasn't until she was being fitted for her wedding dress, which a local dressmaker friend of Janet's was making, that she realised if she didn't do something soon it would be too late.

It wasn't so difficult to find Reece in his office as to catch him there alone. Lately he had been working a lot with Ian, and down in the yard, stripped off with the men. She had become sensitively averse to going there, finding him naked to the waist, sometimes rubbing greasy hands over his broad, dark-haired chest, as if deliberately drawing her attention to his tautly muscled frame. This, and the mocking gaze he would fix on her, almost guaranteed her immediate retreat, and he knew it. The stupid weakness which seized her legs on such occasions, the hot flush which dyed her cheeks, had contributed to her total defeat. Now if there was a message for him she sent it with Ian, or anyone she could get hold of.

One day, however, she managed to get him to herself. Ian was out, so she was hopeful of having an uninterrupted word with Reece.

'It's ridiculous!' she exclaimed, closing the office door firmly and taking up her favourite stand by the window, the view providing a legitimate excuse for looking elsewhere when Reece's all-seeing gaze got too much for her.

'What is?' he asked mildly, scarcely looking up.

'The way I have to almost plan it like a military campaign before I can speak to you privately!'

Obliquely he glanced at her. 'This is your last day here, Zoe, before the wedding. We've both been busy. I've had a lot to sort out, as you know, so I can get away.'

'It's never bothered you quite so much before,' she said sharply.

'I've never had so much on my mind before.'

She didn't pause to consider the odd note in his voice. 'I've a lot on mine, too.'

'And you want to relieve yourself a little?' he observed coolly. 'Do you think I can't guess what's coming? Well, let me tell you, although I realise such advice will be wasted, to save your breath. I've heard it all before and I'm not prepared to listen again while you inform me you don't wish to be married.'

'Well, I don't!' she almost screamed, feeling about two years old under his dismissive eye. How on earth did her senses respond the way they did to such an unfeeling man?

'It's no use, Zoe,' a hush fell on the room as he gazed at her adamantly. 'Why don't you come and sit down?' When she shook her head he went on sternly, 'You can't get out of marrying me without hurting a lot of people, so stop being a selfish little brat and think of others for a change.'

'I am!' her voice rose again in sheer frustration, 'I'm thinking of you.'

'But also of yourself?'

She was, she couldn't deny it. She wondered how

she would be able to face the heartache which lay ahead when Reece grew tired of being tied to a wife he didn't love. But if he wouldn't listen to reason, why should she bother any more?

'I'll just say this,' she cried bitterly, 'you'll be sorry you didn't listen. I'll lead you such a dance . . .!

'You'll be the one who's sorry,' he replied, his mouth tightening warningly as he turned back to his work, 'if you do that.'

The church was crowded for the wedding. Zoe was vaguely aware of what looked like a sea of faces as she walked up the aisle on her grandfather's arm. She wore white and was a beautiful bride. A tear slid down Taggart's cheek as he gently removed her hand from his arm to place it in the one her bridegroom held out to her. Reece gripped it and she met his dark, passionate eyes and saw nothing else. Whatever his true feelings, she realised afterwards, he gave every appearance of being devoted to her that day.

Later they flew to London and then to Mexico City, arriving there in time for breakfast next morning. Zoe had slept on the plane, but she still felt tired and was secretly relieved when Reece said they would have an easy day and that he wasn't meeting Rafael Carrillo until later in the week.

Their hotel was near the U.S. Embassy, a fine modern one, luxuriously furnished with air-conditioning and swimming pools. It appeared to have everything, despite being in the middle of the city. Reece had booked one of its penthouse suites, and Zoe marvelled at such extravagance. She ought to have been impressed, and she was, but she couldn't help thinking nostalgically of Sam Colter's island.

'Like it?' Reece asked, as she wandered around examining every little thing with the round-eyed wonder of a child presented with a set of new toys.

'It's breathtaking!' She glanced at him uncertainly, aware that he was too experienced a traveller to find much novelty in the things she found so incredible. Already, on the way from the International Airport, she had smothered several gasps at the things she had seen. But, if her expression amused him, his eyes were very gentle as he watched her.

He only studied her another second before turning away. 'So you're pleased we came here,' he observed, almost casually.

'Ye—es.'

'Why so hesitant?' He swung back to her so sharply her wits deserted her and she confessed helplessly, 'I— I couldn't help thinking of your boat and Sam Colter's island.'

'You aren't ready for either,' he replied curtly, the tenderness gone from his eyes. 'You wouldn't have appreciated a week of my undivided attention.'

Zoe flushed. 'I hadn't thought of that.'

'What did you think of when you thought of our honeymoon?' There was an unmistakable hint of derision in his voice.

'I hadn't thought about it much,' she muttered evasively, bending her head so he shouldn't see her face. There was a peculiar fluttering in her breast and she didn't want to let him see her eyes. Eyes could reflect too much, she was learning, often more than one wished.

'Wouldn't you like to know my thoughts on the subject?' Reece taunted, his eyes glittering while his mouth twisted in a humourless smile.

'I'm not curious,' she said hastily, feeling suddenly threatened.

'Isn't it about time you were?' He came nearer, his eyes boring into hers. There was a brief gleam of white teeth as they snapped together. His jaw tightened, his eyes hardened and she stared, transfixed. Caught in a flame as he took hold of her, she could feel the heat from it searing through her entire body. It was too late to prevent him seeing something of the intensity of her feelings, and she could only hope he put her quivering reactions down to fright. She was vaguely aware that she mightn't be capable of putting up much fight if Reece decided to make love to her, and she was dismayed that he should have such total control over her emotions.

The magnetic intensity of the gaze he fixed on her had her so much in his power that she actually swayed when he let her go. 'I'll allow you to think that one over,' he said harshly. 'I'm trying to be patient, and we've only just arrived.'

She wasn't sure what he meant by that, she was too busy wrestling with an undefinable disappointment. Her body sagged, sending messages to her brain about being unsatisfied. She tried to ignore it, but felt exhausted from the strain.

Noting it, Reece obviously put it down to tiredness, and insisted she have a rest before lunch.

'The high altitude takes a bit of getting used to. Visitors are advised to have a siesta after lunch for the first few days, but you can have one now, instead. Then, if you like, we can go straight out after we've eaten.'

The suite had two bedrooms. Taking no notice of her ensuing protests, he guided her firmly into one of them. 'You have this,' he said smoothly, 'I'll take the other.'

Until we get used to each other, Zoe supposed, sarcastically, again a vaguely mutinous disappointment tightening the full curves of her lips.

As though to punish her for thoughts he could read plainly and which he knew she would deny if challenged, Reece pushed her far from gently in the direction of the bed and left her. 'I'd have a shower, if I were you,' he said, 'and put on something light, if you have to wear anything at all. And, Zoe . . .' on her way to the bathroom, she stumbled and paused, glancing at him enquiringly, 'separate rooms,' he continued, 'but no closed doors. I don't believe in them between a man and wife.'

Why did he have to be so devilishly enigmatic? Zoe wondered, a few minutes later, as she slid softly between beautiful cool sheets. Before she could decide on an answer, she was asleep.

They ate a late lunch, then went out to explore the city. Having been here before, Reece knew his way round comparatively well. He explained how most of the streets running from east to west were called *avenidas* while those running from north to south were *calles*. Some of the narrower streets, called *callejones*, still retained their old-time cobblestones.

'The Paseo de la Reforma,' he took her there by taxi, 'is one of the most beautiful boulevards in the world.' As they drove a short distance along the eight-mile length of it and Zoe exclaimed at its exceptional width and the way it was shaded by a double line of trees, Reece pointed out the numerous *glorietas*, or circles, many of which contained monuments.

'It seems a beautiful city altogether, if what we've seen so far is anything to go by,' Zoe said enthusiastically, her usual vitality restored by the rest she had had. Not usually caring for cities, she was sure she could come to like this one very much.

'It has a wonderful setting,' Reece's eyes rested appreciatively on her glowing face. 'The city lies in the Valley of Mexico, which is a great basin about sixty miles long by thirty wide, and is surrounded by mountains on all sides except the north. Some of the mountains are volcanic. In the south-east I hope to get the chance of showing you the extinct, snow-capped peaks of twin volcanoes. Popocatepetl and Ixtaccihuatl are both seventeen thousand feet approximately—I forget the exact number of feet, but it will give you some idea of the impressive elevation.'

A little later they left their taxi and walked. Although lying in the tropical belt, the altitude of Mexico City gave it a beautiful climate. 'The days are always pleasant,' Reece told her, as they wandered along, 'though the nights can be very cool. There are only two distinct seasons, the rainy and the dry. The dry season, which my friends here insist is best, is from October to May.'

'So we're lucky, May's only beginning,' Zoe smiled, lifting her face to sunshine which was so much warmer than a normal English spring. It was wonderful, life seemed wonderful, until she remembered the complexities which beset this new marriage of hers. She shivered, and Reece asked if she was cold.

They dined late, as was apparently the custom in most Latin-American countries, and Reece informed her that he always liked to live by the customs of the people whose country he was visiting, if it were possible. Otherwise, he said, one might as well stay at home.

Zoe agreed, although, as she pointed out, this being her first trip abroad, she didn't feel qualified to express a firm opinion on the matter. She wasn't sure whether she was for or against dining late, but she did know she was very hungry indeed long before they sat down.

'Tomorrow, remind me to buy a bar of chocolate or something,' she said, and was rewarded by a wry glance from Reece. 'It's not your tummy that's rumbling!' she hissed, as the waiter approached, and he laughed.

She had bought a new dress for the occasion, a light froth of silky chiffon which had cost far too much. It was incredible how little one got for so much, she thought, viewing herself doubtfully in her bedroom mirror. She had purchased it on impulse, believing it would pack into little space. Its two narrow straps scarcely looked strong enough to support the fragile bodice, and when she turned sideways the tender curve of her breasts were clearly outlined. She didn't feel very happy in it, but it was too late to change. Reece appeared to approve, at any rate.

Throughout dinner he talked lightly and impersonally on many subjects, but there was nothing impersonal in the glance he frequently flicked over her. If he didn't intend claiming his full marital rights, he obviously didn't mean to deprive himself of them all. Zoe drew a breath of what was almost relief when it was time to go back upstairs. A racing pulse, which Reece's calculating stare seemed able to accelerate physically, had her feeling nearly as exhausted as she had been that morning.

In her room she stripped off and took another shower before putting on her nightdress. It had been a present from her grandmother and, like her dress, she had eyed it earlier with some doubt, if for different reasons. Now she dived with relief into its voluminous folds. Reece had already bade her goodnight, but if he did look in—or glance in, as the door was open—she was determined to be decently clad.

To her dismay, he was sitting astride her dressing-table stool as she left her bathroom. He was wearing a short towelling robe and nothing else. When he saw her he threw back his head and laughed. 'You'd pass for a young choirboy in that!'

Zoe stared at him indignantly, raising long-sleeved arms to clutch her high-necked gown even tighter.

'You'll be far too hot.' His laughter faded, although he was obviously having some difficulty in keeping a straight face. 'I must admit I prefer the sort of thing Ursula was wearing, on the night of that party you made a mistake about.'

Zoe might have forgotten her wounded dignity and laughed with him, if he hadn't mentioned Ursula. 'You

can't even forget other women on your wedding night!'
she exclaimed, outraged.

That wiped the smile clean off his face. 'Before you
begin criticising,' he snapped, 'it might pay you to
remember I'm not having a wedding night, not in the
accepted sense of the word.'

Flushing wildly, she glanced at him helplessly,
knowing she was at fault. 'I'm sorry,' she faltered,
wishing she had the courage to go up to him, put her
arms around him and tell him now much she loved
him.

But while she hesitated, he rose to leave, dismissing
her brief apology as if she had never made it. His face
dark, he said icily, 'I confess I was teasing you a little,
and perhaps unkindly, but I don't think it could have
hurt nearly so much as another course of action I might
have resorted to, if you'd been willing.'

CHAPTER NINE

ZOE was surprised when Rafael Carrillo got in touch with Reece the following morning before they left their suite and asked them to dine with his wife and him that evening.

Reece accepted. 'I hope you feel up to it?' His eyebrow quirked as he looked at Zoe. When she frowned uncertainly, he sighed and said, 'I couldn't very well refuse, he's a friend of mine and a very wealthy client. It should be an experience for you, though, a chance to visit a Mexican household and see how they live.'

'Won't his wife mind entertaining a stranger?'

'She's used to it,' Reece smiled, with an air of reminiscence about him which Zoe didn't think about until afterwards. 'You'll like her, she's very charming.'

Despite her first misgivings, Zoe found herself looking forward to it, until she actually met Dolores Carrillo and saw how very beautiful she was.

Señora Carrillo obviously knew Reece well. 'Ah, Reece,' she pronounced his name with half a dozen e's, 'so you have choosen a wife at last, but why one so young?'

'She is older than she looks.' Reece kissed the delightful Dolores on both cheeks, taking, Zoe considered, his time over it.

'All of seventeen?'

'Almost twenty.' Reece retained his grip on Zoe's balled hand while continuing to smile at the lovely Señora.

Rafael Carrillo, to whom Zoe had already been introduced, was called to the telephone, and Dolores said something very quickly to Reece in Spanish. Reece replied briefly in the same language and Zoe was dismayed by the flash of something intimate between them. Was this yet another woman from Reece's past? she wondered unhappily.

Dolores didn't speak to Reece again in Spanish and, as if to make up for her first moments of neglect, was charming to Zoe throughout the evening. She and her husband were nearer Reece's age than Zoe's, and Zoe hadn't realised they were such close friends. But there was much talk and laughter in which she was included, and soon she forgot her former animosity, although there still remained a disquieting niggle.

The Carrillos had a beautiful home on the outskirts of the city. Zoe was shown round it before dinner, a trip which included a peep in the nursery, since Rafael and Dolores had three children.

'Do you like children?' Dolores asked.

Reece was out of earshot so didn't see Zoe's cheeks colour faintly as she nodded her head. 'I'd love several,' she said, 'as I'm an only child myself.'

'You will have to speak to Reece, then,' Dolores smiled, her voice equally low, 'I'm sure he will be only too willing to oblige.'

It wasn't the last time that evening that Zoe felt slightly embarrassed by something Dolores said, but she soon discovered it was more a difference in outlook than a deliberate attempt to make her feel uncomfortable. In Mexico, she soon gathered, children were a very important part of family life and no marriage was considered complete without them.

Señor Carrillo was as charming as his wife and as talkative, but Zoe thought he looked tired. During dinner, a typical Mexican meal and served late as was the custom, he told Zoe much about Mexico's past history and a little of its people. She was surprised to learn that less than a million were of purely Spanish descent, while half the remainder were Indian and the rest a mixture of Indian and Spaniard. And while English was spoken, the language generally was Spanish.

Altogether it was a very pleasant evening, and before they left Señor Carrillo arranged to take them on a sightseeing tour next day. He would have liked them to spend some time with him and his family at the coast where, he assured Zoe, as Reece knew, they had a splendid house. Reece said regretfully that it would have been a pleasure had they not had to return home.

Reece had hired a car and they drove back to their hotel in it. In their suite again, Zoe asked a little indignantly, 'We only have a few days, do we have to spend them with other people?'

As she spoke she began throwing off her light wrap and unzipping her dress. Reece hadn't touched her since they were married, which made her feel confident he never would. When Dolores had talked of children Zoe could have laughed. Reece wandered around their suite, often without giving her a second glance.

He rather threw her off balance now by exclaiming savagely, 'Do you think if we'd been having a proper honeymoon, I'd have agreed to spending any of it with other people?'

'Oh, I don't really mind,' she said hurriedly, apprehensive of a change in the atmosphere she didn't understand. Turning towards him, she smiled appealingly in an attempt to get rid of the sudden tension, and as she did so her dress, which she had momentarily forgotten she had unfastened, fell to the ground about her feet. Gasping, she stumbled and would have fallen if Reece hadn't caught her.

'Can't you watch what you're doing!' he snapped tersely.

She stiffened, but his body was pressed against her own and in her legs was the old familiar weakness. Depleted of her dress, she was left standing in only her panties, and a bra which revealed more than it concealed of her full, young figure. 'Oh, God, you're so beautiful,' he groaned, pulling her closer, so she could feel the mounting tension in him.

'But not as beautiful as Dolores Carrillo?' she taunted, desperately seeking any way she could think of to avoid falling into the abyss which seemed to be yawning with her dress at her feet.

Blue eyes glittered down on her before a dark head bent and hard, punishing lips descended on her own. For long seconds the room spun dizzily as she clung to him yet tried to fight the desire which she felt surging through her. She was fully aware he was making her suffer for her remark, but her defences against him seemed to be dwindling by the minute.

His hands slid up her arm in a feather-light caress to her shoulders. 'Dolores,' he muttered thickly, 'doesn't appeal to me the way you do.'

His mouth came down again and she gasped as his hands began touching her intimately, while the treacherous weakness sweeping through her body was making her tremblingly conscious of her own vulnerability. As her mouth opened under his, she was possessed of a craving so strong, it rendered her almost mindless in his embrace.

Reece lifted his head and she watched his face with a kind of dreamy wonder. He might have been having some sort of struggle with himself, she couldn't be sure, because everything was hazy.

She heard him sigh and mutter something roughly as his mouth roamed over her cheek, bit into her ear, bruised the soft skin of her neck. With an urgent restlessness his hands circled her slender back, then followed the slight curve of her hips to shape her unresistingly to him.

During the years she had known Reece she had often driven him too far and been frightened by his anger. This evening she had provoked him, but the fright within her was a different kind, for she hadn't been in

love with him before. Brought up against the hardening
contours of his aroused male body, she began trembling
in earnest, sensing he was tempted to chastise her but not,
as was his usual fashion, with a few sharp words.

Lifting weighted lashes to gaze at him, she was
struck by the harsh indecision on his face. With a pro-
testing murmur she fastened her arms compulsively
about his waist. Afterwards, vaguely able to retrace the
course of her actions, she wondered how far her wanton
demonstration of her reluctance to let him go had in-
fluenced his next move. Might he not have just flung
her from him if she hadn't so fiercely hung on to him?
If she had whispered even one small word of protest,
would he have picked her up with a defeated groan
and carried her to his bed?

'It had to happen some time, I suppose,' he
murmured huskily, laying her down.

Her eyes were locked in his as he threw off his
clothes. Something wordless winged between them and
though she didn't realise its significance she began to
quiver. The emotions struggling within her were
clearly reflected on her feverish face and a ghost of a
reassuring smile played on Reece's mouth while his
eyes studied her darkly.

'I don't want to hurt you,' he said thickly as he came
down beside her, taking her in his arms again.

Zoe wished he hadn't spoken. He had jerked her
from her dream world to a realisation of what she was
inviting. Hurt often was born of hate, and that was all
he felt for her. All he could feel for her after being
forced into marrying her. Wondering how she could so
easily have forgotten, she began struggling wildly.

'It's too late, my darling!' Contempt dried his voice
to a hoarse whisper as he refused to allow her to escape
from him. There was no gentleness in the mouth which
touched hers, then kissed her throat before continuing
a devastating path downwards.

Her resistance collapsed. A whisper of it lingered, then was gone as her tenseness relaxed. Flames licked through her veins as his hands and mouth went over her, leaving little of her unexplored. Her senses clamoured while her heart raced like a forest fire out of control.

'You're so warm and soft and beautiful,' he murmured, and his return to tenderness proved her final undoing. With a little moan she clung to him, surrendering completely to the desire blazing within her.

As his arms tightened on her yielding body she submissively obeyed his silent commands. He was using his mouth with a sure expertise, arousing her to the point of complete capitulation, and she was like a puppet, alive and wholly responsive to his every move. Pain and passion inevitably blended, flung together in a turmoil of seething emotions, one seeming to be fighting the other until passion finally won. As they slid from the last area of nebulous awareness, she whimpered at the strength with which Reece held her to him. No words could have expressed how she felt as the sweetly ravishing torture of his complete possession vibrated through her entire being, flooding her, after the next fleeting few moments, with a rapturous, mindless ecstasy.

They spent the following day with the Carrillos, and the next two alone before returning home, but Reece didn't make love to her again. In fact he treated her exactly as if nothing had happened, and as she had woken the next morning in her own bed, she was apt to wonder if anything really had. How she had got back to her own bed she had not yet found the courage to ask, for she sensed the answer to such a query might embarrass her more than Reece. She could imagine him carrying her there, his hard eyes contemplating and cynical before he covered her up and put out the light.

The day they spent with his friends had provided a welcome breathing space, she had to admit. Despite still being jealous of the attention Reece showered on Dolores, Zoe found it easier to be with other people, and was almost glad when he kept his distance. She wasn't sure what Rafael Carrillo had thought of them, a newly married couple who treated each other as strangers, but she had been too unhappy to really care.

It wasn't until they were on the plane coming home that Reece had explained about the Carrillos.

'Shall I tell you the truth about them?' he asked, taking her hand and holding it lightly.

This intimate action, after he had been unfriendly for days, confused her. She said stiffly, although she was dying to know, 'If you like.'

His cynical glance told her he was quite aware of the curiosity she was doing her best to hide, nevertheless, he didn't attempt to punish her by changing his mind.

'I went to university with Rafael,' he said, his voice so bleak that Zoe was surprised. 'We became good friends,' he went on, 'and I was invited to his wedding. His marriage was an arranged one, but he and Dolores were—still are, for that matter—very much in love. Unfortunately, over recent years, he has developed a serious heart condition and has been advised not to travel. But because I didn't get to see him a few weeks ago, he decided he would come and see me. Dolores rang and told me how dangerous it would be for him to come to Scotland, so I arranged instead to visit him on our honeymoon. When she spoke to me in Spanish it was because she was so upset. She was merely telling me quickly that there had been no improvement since we'd talked over the phone.'

'I'm sorry, Reece.' After a horrified moment, Zoe found her voice while her green eyes darkened with dismay. Blindly she stared through the cabin window, seeing something of the heartache of other people which is so often hidden from the casual observer. No one could doubt Rafael Carrillo was a very nice man—

even if he hadn't been, a bad heart was not something
one would wish on anybody, but she felt resentful that
Reece had said nothing until now.

'Why didn't you tell me?' she asked, turning back to
him with a frown.

'I might have done,' he said curtly, 'if you hadn't
been jealous.'

About to deny it loudly, Zoe hesitated. 'All right,'
she retorted, wearily defiant, 'what if I was? I think I
understand now about you and Dolores, but at the time
how was I to know? And is jealousy a crime?'

Reece's eyes glittered angrily as he almost threw her
hand away. 'In this case I think it was. You were jealous
because you thought someone wanted something you
didn't want yourself.'

'So that's why you punished me as you did?' she
said slowly, curiously shocked.

'If you choose to call it punishment.'

Her cheeks burned. 'I can't think of it as anything else.'

'Punishment,' he jeered coldly, 'is rarely something
one enjoys.'

'I didn't!' she denied, too hotly.

'I was there, remember?' His eyes held and taunted
her wild ones, daring her to deny the feelings she had
experienced in his arms. 'You responded too well not
to have enjoyed it.'

She felt sickened, though why she should be she
wasn't sure. Reece was used to chastising her. That
she was now his wife wouldn't alter such a firmly
established habit. He must never know how much she
loved him as this would merely provide him with another means of hurting her when she annoyed him.
Already he had too many.

'Well, you've had your revenge,' she strove to speak
lightly, 'but I hope it doesn't happen again. I'm sure
neither of us enjoyed it all that much.'

'You're my wife, Zoe,' he replied, so mockingly she

couldn't fail to understand him. 'Why should a man keep a wife and have to seek his entertainment elsewhere?'

Reece was never crude. He might be bad-tempered and arrogant, but never that. That he appeared to be now frightened her—this, and the funny white ring round his mouth. Her senses reeling, she gasped the first thing to enter her head, 'You have Ursula. Don't forget your parents would have preferred her for a daughter-in-law.'

'Indeed?' he retorted suavely, his eyes cold, 'I suppose she's always someone I can keep in mind, for when I grow tired of you.'

They arrived home early on Friday evening, having had little more to say to each other. They had driven in a taxi from the airstrip and, as it dropped them at the house and left, Reece turned to her. 'This will give us time to get ourselves sorted out before Monday.'

Zoe wasn't sure what to make of that, so she merely nodded.

'It will also give us a chance to look over the house,' he said.

She paused, glancing up at it apprehensively. Everything was changing too fast for her, she didn't know how to cope. She felt she was on a merry-go-round and if she didn't do something to stop it, it never would.

'I don't want the house altered,' she whispered. 'I thought I'd told you?'

Reece ignored this coolly. 'For quite a while I've been thinking of a few things I'd like changed myself, only it didn't seem worth the effort and I was busy building up the yard. Now, however, the situation has changed. I have a wife to think of and, in the not too distant future, I hope a family.'

'A family?' Her eyes flew from their study of bricks and mortar to his face.

'Don't look so stunned,' he taunted. 'Did you imagine I wouldn't want one?'

She floundered, scuffing her toe in the gravel while trying to control her racing pulses. 'With things as they are between us can you wonder?'

His voice was clipped. 'You've known me a long time, Zoe, you must have realised I'm fond of children?'

'You were never very fond of me!'

He grinned suddenly, as she reminded him. 'You didn't make it easy for me to love you then,' he said enigmatically, 'but I used to put up with having you around when you did nothing but get in the way.'

When he used the word love, she shivered and decided they were on dangerous ground. Quickly she turned to leave him, running with fleet feet up the grey stone steps to the front door. She felt choked with misery, but managed to say carelessly, 'Your trouble is, Reece Macadam, you talk too much.'

For an answer he swung her high in his arms, the devil glinting from his dark eyes as he held her tightly while inserting the key. As the door swung open he carried her through it, to the accompaniment of his growling, threatening laughter. 'I can assure you, my young madam,' he taunted, 'there'll be times when I won't talk at all.'

As he set her down with a punishing thump she was so shaken she swayed. 'What was all that about?' she asked angrily.

'Oh, just for the benefit of the neighbours,' he grinned. 'It's traditional, you know.'

Zoe wondered how he could stand there and smile with so little amusement. But she had seen him at it before, in the office, the boatyard, where it had usually presaged a storm. 'We haven't any neighbours!' she hissed.

'Are you using the royal "we"?' he jeered sarcastically, 'or do you really feel you belong here at last?'

'You're just about impossible!' she snapped, her face flushed.

'Well, whatever your opinion of me,' Reece said

indifferently, 'I'm going to make a cup of tea. Unless you'd prefer a drink why not join me? If nothing else it might improve your temper.'

It was several minutes before she could bring herself to do as he suggested, and then it was only because she had no wish to appear to be childishly sulking in the hall. It might be more dignified to pretend nothing had happened. Reece was in a funny mood, not one she wholly recognised. It might pay her to be careful.

Sitting down at the kitchen table, she drank the mug of tea he pushed towards her and looked at him. A strand of pale hair fell over her shoulder and her eyes were very green. 'I'd like to go straight to my room and have a bath or a shower, then I'll come down and start dinner.'

'Just as you like,' he agreed briefly, his eyes lingering on her over the rim of his own mug.

Unable to sit still under his close scrutiny, she got up again, her mind working with difficulty. He had told her there was plenty of stuff in the fridge and deep freeze. The central heating was on taking care of the hot water. Did he have any milk? When she asked him, and he flicked a quick glance at the almost full bottle on the sink, she flushed. 'Of course,' she muttered. 'Stupid of me.'

'You've travelled a long way,' he remarked, in a tone of voice which seemed to add to her confusion. As she returned to the table her hand caught her mug, knocking it over.

'Oh!' she cried, ready to burst into tears. 'It's all your fault!'

'Indeed?'

Reece was on his high horse again, all raised brows and cool condescension. Zoe flashed him another glance of sheer hatred and began mopping desperately at the spilt tea with a cloth.

'I'm going upstairs,' she babbled. 'There'll be beds to make up, then I'll take a shower.'

'A good idea,' he said coolly. 'It will calm you down.'

Thinking he was having another dig at her temper, she retorted sharply, 'I'm not angry.'

'Just very tense,' he amended, with a slight twist of his lips. 'But then you've always been capable of getting into a state over nothing. Go upstairs and have your bath, then you'll feel better.'

'You will be busy down here?' she asked pointedly, forgetting she had been going to do everything herself.

'Of course,' he replied, as though he had no idea it was a hint that she didn't wish to be followed.

She was behaving stupidly, she told herself, clutching her overnight bag and hurrying into the bathroom, which she remembered from the time he was ill was opposite Reece's bedroom. Closing the door and bolting it, she tugged off her sticky clothes and soaked in the bath for ages. It was lovely and warm and as the tension seeped slowly out of her she knew she was glad to be home. Suddenly, as she relaxed, the future didn't look so bleak any more. Reece wasn't easy to understand, but between the two of them it should be possible to work something out.

Reassured by such thoughts, she pulled the plug out of the bath and began drying herself. Not until then did she remember she had brought no fresh clothes to put on. In her overnight case was only the thin robe which Reece had bought her, along with other things in Mexico City. Rather than go naked, or wear her stale clothes again, she shrugged her damp body into this. She hadn't worn it before as she had had her own bathroom in the hotel and hadn't felt any need of it. The night attire Gran had given her had covered her more than adequately. Now she regarded the robe's semi-transparency doubtfully and tied the sash even tighter about her narrow waist.

Outside, in the corridor, she paused to consider the various rooms. There was the one Reece occupied and several more. After a moment she decided the third one along would do nicely, not too near yet not too far. He couldn't complain that she was interfering with his privacy or trying to remove herself completely. Resolutely she walked to the door of the third room and looked in.

It was very nice, a big square room with a large bed and a good view—what more could she want? A lot more, a niggling little voice inside her suggested, but firmly she ignored it. Dropping the bag she carried on the floor, she opened the window, then returned to the corridor to get some clean sheets from the linen cupboard at the other end of it.

She had the sheets on the bed and was busy with the pillow-slips when Reece entered.

'What the hell do you think you're doing?' he asked grimly.

'Making my bed.' She pushed back the heavy swathe of hair which wouldn't seem to keep in place this evening, without looking at him. 'What did you think I was doing?'

'You aren't sleeping here,' he snapped, his mouth thinning at her defiant tone. 'You're sleeping with me.'

Dropping the pillow she was holding, Zoe glanced at him nervously, apprehensive of the way he spelt every word of his last sentence out. 'We—we had separate rooms at the hotel . . .'

'But this isn't a hotel,' he said brusquely, 'and we've been married over a week.' His dark blue eyes took in her heightening colour then wandered deliberately over her body, lingering on the rounded swell of her breasts, the curve of her hips, the smooth, slender legs clearly defined by the thin robe she was wearing. 'That was then, not now, and I mean to start as I intend to go on.'

'No!' Fright suddenly galvanised her into action, releasing her from a temporary incapability to move. As Reece advanced grimly towards her she twisted away from him. She must have moved too soon or too quickly as she seemed to trip over her feet. It might have been a bump in the carpet, she never knew, but she would have fallen if Reece hadn't caught her. He held her firmly and so closely that she trembled. She could feel the whole length of him, his well muscled back, the hardness of his broad chest, the intense, overpowering maleness which she was just beginning to realise was so much a part of him. She shivered uncontrollably and the world seemed to break into a kaleidoscope of colour.

'Please, Reece,' she begged hoarsely, making a desperate effort to gather her scattered wits, 'Let's talk this thing over sensibly.'

He dismissed the mute appeal in her face and instead of releasing her he picked her up. With a last harsh glance around, he turned, making for the door, carrying her ruthlessly back to his room. How well she remembered it—the big bed, the big furniture, the wide windows through which the last rays of the setting sun were dazzling her dazed eyes.

He dropped her on the bed, but her release was only momentary. Swiftly he came down beside her, pulling her close again, moulding her soft curves against him until she cried out from a kind of enchanted anguish. He sighed unsteadily, muttering something under his breath as he bent his head to find her mouth. It was a light touch at first, until response flooded through her, shaking her with an intensity of feeling such as she had never known, then the pressure of his lips increased and she was helplessly at the mercy of a shattering excitement which grew by the minute beyond her control.

Zoe shuddered, struggling for words as he raised himself fractionally to gaze down on her.

'Don't talk,' he said thickly. 'We've done too much talking already. We'll try this way for a change.'

Slowly he ran his hand through the thick fall of her

hair, the hollow of her cheek. Expertly he began releasing the tortured ties at her waist, and, as her robe parted his hand rested on the bare contours of her slender body. Her gaze clung to him as a flicker of fear shivered through her.

'Don't,' she entreated.

Reece answered with his mouth. It met hers, crushing away her remaining resistance while his hands continued their remorseless exploration. Zoe's senses began to soar while the room about her dimmed and vanished. Wherever he touched he aroused flames which seemed to join to make a blazing fire. Her mind swung dizzily, blanking out rational thought until she was clinging to him wildly, overwhelmed by a physical craving so strong it brought her to the verge of surrender. Her former apprehension of his passion faded and she wanted to know again the sensuous delight she had already shared with him.

'Zoe?' he murmured, taking his mouth from hers, whispering her name.

His voice was rough and she recognised the question in it. He wanted her and was controlling himself long enough to ask her permission. She suspected he would plunder and take, whether she gave her permission or not, but knew she couldn't deny that she wanted him as much as he wanted her.

Convulsively she moaned and swallowed, her arms going tightly around his neck, while her reply was lost against his lips. In the moistness of her mouth she heard his sigh of satisfaction, a sound which seemed to vibrate through her entire body.

'I've got too many clothes on,' he groaned impatiently, beginning to unbuckle his belt.

The back of his knuckles digging into her as he did so only seemed to heighten the other sensations shooting through her, but the slight pause gave her a moment to strive for sanity. 'Reece,' she gasped, 'I was going to cook dinner.'

'Who wants to eat?' he muttered thickly, his mouth moving from the delicate lobe of her ear to the softly tinted orb of her breast. 'This is all I'll ever need.'

It was then that the doorbell rang, again and again. As the peals of it vibrated through the house, Reece groaned and lifted a reluctant head. 'Go away!' he shouted angrily.

Whoever it was didn't. The insistent chimes went on, indicating that the person on the doorstep might possess more than a fair share of determination. Reece's arms tightened around Zoe's ardent but stiffening body, then with a smothered curse he rolled away from her. His face was tense, but he didn't appear at all embarrassed as he dressed himself swiftly before her drugged gaze.

'Your eyes go a curious shade of green when I make love to you,' he said gently, pausing to bend over her to watch the soft flush tint her paling cheeks before he walked away.

'I'll go and see who our visitor is,' he drawled derisively. 'Stay where you are, I won't be long.'

His tone of voice, suggesting as it did that he would be more than willing to murder whoever it was he found when he answered the door, filled Zoe with apprehension. It might be her grandparents, although she very much doubted it, but if it was she hoped Reece wouldn't be rude to them.

Scrambling off the bed wasn't easy, not when her legs still felt weak. Zoe wasn't conscious of reaching the window, but she made it. She took a few deep breaths, trying to throw off the almost catastrophic effects of Reece's lovemaking while staring down on the drive below. A small car was parked there, and she immediately recognised it as the one Ursula Findlay usually drove.

The bedroom wasn't directly above the front door

but more to the side of it. By craning her neck she was just able to see Ursula's elegant figure and hear her delighted laughter as Reece opened the door. What could she want? Zoe wondered, her spirits plummeting. She might have been happy to see someone, especially if it meant Reece would be diverted, but never Ursula.

If Reece had been furious when he left her, he had apparently recovered very quickly. As she heard the two below laughing and talking together, Zoe's heart was suddenly aching. What a tragedy if Reece had been forced to marry her while still loving Ursula! It had always been difficult to read his mind, but it was obvious he had feelings for Ursula of some kind. Right at this moment he could be wishing he was married to her, instead of Zoe Kerr.

Zoe dressed slowly, knowing he wouldn't be back, and followed him unhappily downstairs. She felt confused and her thoughts clung to the warm room she had just left. Why did she let Reece tear her in two as he did? One part of her had wanted to surrender to his expert seduction, while the other fought consistently against belonging to him without love. She was a fool, she knew, to go on hoping that one day he might come to love her as she loved him. Only fools, she told herself scornfully, really believed in happy endings.

She found them in the kitchen, where Ursula seemed remarkably at home. She was unpacking a large box of provisions while Reece half sat on the edge of the table watching her.

'Hello, Zoe.' Ursula glanced up, smiling brightly; she might easily have been the mistress of the house instead of Zoe. 'I heard you were back, so I brought you something to eat—a welcome home present, if you like. Aunt Fiona, Reece's mother, you know, said it was more than likely that you'd forget to get anything in.'

'We have enough.' Zoe stubbornly ignored Reece's

frowning glance. 'And we could have gone out,' she added belligerently, not over-concerned that she might sound ill-mannered.

'It was good of you to go to so much trouble, anyway,' soothed Reece, the eyes which lingered on his wife turning icy.

'Perhaps you'd care to stay and join us for dinner?' Zoe suggested quickly, with the innocent air of one truly repentant for her unintentional rudeness. She wasn't sure what was driving her. It must be the look in Reece's eyes which spoke of utter dislike. Obviously he was regretting the interlude they had just shared upstairs as bitterly as she was.

Vaguely she was aware of Ursula almost purring and saying she would be delighted to stay—and was there anything she could do to help? And of Reece, replying tersely that he was sure Zoe preferred to manage on her own, and it might be a better idea if Ursula and he retired to the lounge and had a drink.

So it happened that while Zoe spent the next hour or so slaving in the kitchen, Reece, without another glance, escorted Ursula out of sight. Zoe truculently wished she had poisoned the sherry. A little later she heard them wandering around the hall before going out into the grounds. Reece was talking of the alterations he intended doing, something Zoe had fully expected him to discuss with her. This seemed to confirm her suspicions that he was thinking seriously about a divorce, and that remarriage was what he had in mind when he showed Ursula so painstakingly over the house.

CHAPTER TEN

URSULA stayed quite late, until no one in fact appeared to have anything left to say, and the music Reece played sounded more like a dirge than pleasurable entertainment. And when she did eventually go and Zoe stubbornly returned to the room she had first prepared for herself, Reece made no further attempts to persuade her to change her mind about sleeping with him. Going to his own room, he closed the door sharply, which somehow seemed to put an end to all Zoe's hopes for the future.

The next morning, as she came downstairs, the telephone rang and, as Reece came out of the kitchen and crossed the hall to his study to answer it, she heard him muttering something about there being no escape from anything or anyone.

In the kitchen she found coffee already made and bacon frying. As Reece returned and she began apologising for being late, he interrupted abruptly,

'You cooked our dinner last night, so it was only fair.' Without glancing at her again, he sat down and went on to mention briefly that it had been Ian on the phone. There was some kind of trouble at the yard and he would have to go immediately after breakfast.

Zoe poured his coffee and glanced at him anxiously as he ate his bacon and eggs. 'Will you be gone long? Shall I come with you?'

'No,' he replied curtly. 'And I may be gone for hours. We aren't very big, but you know what it is when there's even a small dispute to settle.' When Zoe merely said yes, in a voice she didn't realise was so desolate, he looked up with a frown. 'It's not much of a homecoming for you, I'm afraid—an unexpected guest last night and more trouble this morning.'

She wasn't sure what he meant by that, but at least he was trying to be friendlier. After Ursula left, the evening before, he had scarcely spoken to her. However, if he could make an effort, so must she. 'Things seldom go according to plan,' she remarked, rather tritely, 'but we have the rest of the weekend.'

'Oh, that reminds me,' with a quick glance at his watch, Reece rose from the table, 'Ursula's parents are giving a party tonight and I promised we'd look in. After all, we have nothing else to do.'

Zoe felt stunned. 'How do you know it's not another hoax?' she gasped.

'She assures me it isn't. What an unforgiving child you are,' he jeered coldly. 'Don't you ever forget anything?'

In a kind of daze, Zoe watched while he gathered a few things together. When he was ready to go, he glanced over his shoulder, apparently to say goodbye, then swung round abruptly, his eyes narrowed on her colourless face.

'Are you feeling all right?' he demanded.

'Yes . . . Why?'

'You don't look it,' his voice hardened. 'Do you find being married to me so upsetting?'

Bleakly she shook her head, so that her hair like a cloud hid her face.

She heard his terse sigh. 'Perhaps it's fresh air you need after flying most of yesterday. Why don't you go out and get some.?

'I don't need fresh air,' she replied, then added desperately, because she couldn't forget it, 'If you think I need that why did you promise to go to Ursula's party?'

His voice went cold. 'You don't have to go.'

Incredulously she whispered, 'You mean you'd go

yourself and leave me here?'

'Would you mind?'

She lifted her head to stare at him, and because she looked closely for the first time, she saw the dark smudges under his eyes, the haggard lines running from mouth to nose. 'You love her, don't you?' she said simply.

Reece jerked upright, as though he'd been shot, then the telephone rang again. In a kind of bewildered daze, Zoe followed him into the study and noticed his hand was shaking as he picked up the receiver. It was a wrong number this time, but it seemed to remind him of his obligations.

'I can't talk now, Zoe,' his face was no less grim than his voice as his eyes rested on her hovering figure. 'I believe there's something you should know, but Ian Graham's waiting, and what I have to say is too important to say in a hurry.'

'Yes,' she murmured dully, tears stinging her eyes as she walked to the door with him. 'Reece,' she called on impulse, as he ran down the steps, 'if you don't want me at the office, would you mind if I went to see my grandparents?'

Pausing, he shook his head. 'If you come now, I'll drop you off,' he offered.

'No,' she replied, careful to keep her voice from trembling. 'It's too early and I'd as soon walk. You go ahead.'

But as soon as he had gone Zoe knew she had to get out of the house. If she didn't she was going to break down and sob, and Reece would know when he came home as her eyes would be red. He must want to discuss a divorce. Probably not an immediate one—he wasn't that cruel, at least he wouldn't want to think he was. She imagined he would allow a decent interval to go by before they parted, but he would divorce her and marry Ursula. He would insist he had done as much as could be expected, and being divorced was no disgrace. That her reputation would have suffered far more if she had remained single and it had become known how she had spent the night alone with him on Sam Colter's island.

Quickly, because she hated to leave an untidy kitchen, she rinsed their breakfast things and put them away. As she did so she was surprised to notice that Reece had scarcely touched his breakfast. He must be more concerned than he had appeared to be about the trouble at the yard. She began to be actively worried herself and wondered what could be wrong. The men were usually so good, and it wasn't as if Reece hadn't been away before. Perhaps her grandfather would know something? After shaking the cushions up in the lounge and opening the windows, she set off for the town without even bothering to run upstairs and fetch a jacket.

Taggart and Janet were surprised to see her, and even more surprised that she had arrived alone. 'We didn't expect to see you so soon,' Janet exclaimed, as Zoe kissed them both warmly. 'Where's Reece?'

While Zoe explained, she watched her grandfather closely. 'Ian Graham rang, and I don't think he would have if it had just been something trivial.'

'I've only been to the boatyard once while you've been away,' said Taggart when she finished speaking, 'I suppose I didn't want your husband to think I was snooping around as soon as his back was turned. All I've heard are one or two rumours, and you know how distorted gossip can get. For what it's worth, I believe there has been trouble, but more from outside interference than anything else, and that's all I'm going to say.'

'Reece won't be in any danger?' Zoe's face went so white, Taggart gazed at her in alarm. Men in these parts would never be reduced to tame robots, and as

many arguments were still settled by what Zoe chose
to consider physical violence as were brought to a
satisfactory conclusion around a table.

'No,' Taggart put his arm around her affectionately
and shook his head. 'There's nothing, I'm very sure
that Reece won't be able to handle. And if you don't
believe that,' he chuckled dryly, 'you've got a very
short memory!'

It seemed she wasn't going to get anything more out
of her grandfather, so she didn't persist. Yet she felt
too uneasy to settle, despite his assurances. She stayed
an hour, drinking the tea Janet made and telling them
about Mexico City. Then she decided she must go
home again and wandered back through the town. She
had to forcibly restrain herself from going to make sure
with her own eyes that Reece was quite safe. Emotion
seemed to be running through her in great waves, so
she wasn't really quite sure what she was doing. The
pain and desire, the unhappiness and odd moments of
joy she had experienced over the last months, were all
part, she was beginning to realise, of loving him.

The morning had grown steadily colder. The wind
was freshening. As she loitered by the harbour Zoe
saw the sea was quite choppy. There weren't many
people about as it was still early, but several boats were
preparing to go out. She watched for a short while and
was just turning away when Ursula came up to her.

'Hello, Zoe,' she exclaimed. 'How nice to see you.'

If you say that once more I'll scream! Zoe found
herself thinking. If she was surprised by her thoughts,
she was even more startled to hear her voice challenging Ursula coldly. 'Why not say something you mean
for a change? I don't think you've ever been pleased to
see me.'

If she had decided to lay her cards on the table,
Ursula was apparently quite willing to follow suit.
'Why should I be?' she sneered. 'You've always been a

little troublemaker. If it hadn't been for you I'd have been Reece's wife long ago. I don't like you, it's only for his sake that I'm trying to be polite, but, as you say, why pretend?'

Zoe gazed at her steadily, seeing the other girl's mature good looks and wondering how she had ever come to believe Reece had grown tired of her.

'I'm sorry,' she muttered, aware that she might have something to apologise for.

'So you should be!' Ursula smiled charmingly at a passing acquaintance but spoke sharply to Zoe. 'You managed to persuade Reece to marry you, something we all know he felt obliged to do, but he is going to divorce you, be in no doubt about that! And when he's married to me I'll make very sure he has nothing whatsoever to do with you again. I'm afraid you'll have to look for employment elsewhere.'

Zoe fought with a despair which made her feel almost ill. Ursula had merely put into words what she had expected to hear from Reece but the shock was great, nonetheless. She swayed and might have fallen if a voice hadn't called her name, jerking her to her senses.

'Zoe!'

Dazed, she glanced over the side of the quay, down to the water. She hadn't heard Freddy Vintis come alongside. He was at the helm of a speedboat and she wondered apprehensively if he could handle it. He appeared to know Ursula, because he grinned and sketched a brief salute, but it was to Zoe he spoke.

'If you aren't doing anything why not come out for a spin? She's a real beaut!'

Zoe's first inclination was to refuse, then she paused. Why shouldn't she go out with Freddy? If Reece thought other men liked her, his conscience might not trouble him so much.

As she hesitated, Ursula laid a light hand on her

arm, as though she and Zoe were the best of friends. 'What will Reece have to say when he hears you've run off with his bride, Mr Vintis?' she teased.

'Are you going to tell him?' Freddy laughed, as if he wished she would.

'I might,' Ursula laughed back, while glancing mockingly at Zoe's uncertain face. 'Are you scared?' she taunted the younger girl softly.

'You can tell him what you like,' Zoe muttered, uncaringly. Would it matter what Reece believed? Perhaps she should give him good reason to seek a divorce. Going out with Freddy Vintis, whom he disliked, might make a start.

'Are you scared?' she heard Freddy repeating Ursula's challenge in the same mocking tones and was quite aware that he was daring her to go with him. Why he was trying so hard puzzled her, but she felt too heartbroken over what Ursula had just told her to look closely for reasons.

'No, of course not,' she replied, and, without pausing to consider another moment, climbed recklessly down the iron ladder on the side of the quay. Freddy held out his arms and she heard the gasps of people standing nearby as she landed in them. Then she was safely in the boat beside him and they were away.

The boat was more powerful than she had thought and it didn't take her many minutes to realise Freddy hadn't enough experience to be in charge of anything remotely like it.

'Does it belong to you?' she shouted, above the noise of the engines.

'Sure!' he laughed wildly. 'The old man had it sent up. I got fed up waiting for the one your husband's supposed to be building.'

Zoe could have answered that such things take time, time Freddy might well have spent learning something of proper seamanship. He was reckless and she guessed he would be careless of his own safety and that of any passenger he had on board. Yet she couldn't seem to find the will to rebuke him. What did it matter if he drowned them both? What did she have left to live for?

Of course there were her grandparents. She had to remember them, even if Reece no longer wanted her. 'Not so much throttle!' she advised Freddy anxiously, wishing he would let her take over.

'Don't be daft, darling,' Freddy shouted back, 'I'm not even trying. Wait until we get farther out, then I'll really show you what she can do.'

For the first time, Zoe realised just how foolhardy she had been to accept his invitation. 'I think I'd like to go back,' she yelled in his ear. 'I've changed my mind.'

'You might have, darling,' he retorted, 'but I haven't. Apart from the boat, I'm enjoying your company. I still fancy you, and you're married.'

Zoe frowned. 'Yes, I'm married!'

'Just married.'

'What difference does that make?'

'Newly married people are usually very much in love.'

Zoe stared at him. If he thought that, she wasn't going to deny it, but he was grinning devilishly now, and her eyes widened. This was no idle flip around the harbour. Freddy's good mood was gone and, as her glance swung round, she saw they were heading for the open sea. He sent the powerboat crashing into the trough of a wave, drenching them both with spray and jarring their bodies. Such a jolt, she knew, strained a boat's fixtures and could seriously damage a vessel or injure those on board. He was acting like an overgrown schoolboy, but she felt a real sense of dread.

'Perhaps you'd better explain?' she tried to speak coolly and calmly, when she recovered her breath.

'Why are you doing this?'

'Revenge!' He threw back his soaked hair gleefully, 'What did you think? No one dresses me down the way your husband did, this morning, in front of a gang of men and gets away with it. He'll be lucky to get you back in one piece, or even alive, and that's a promise!'

Zoe couldn't believe it. She didn't know Freddy Vintis well, but she could have sworn he was harmless enough. Now his face was darkly vindictive and she was suddenly very much afraid.

'Wait until Miss Findlay tells him where you are, then we'll see some fun,' Freddy chortled. 'When he comes after you he'll have to apologise on his bended knees, unless he wants to see you thrown overboard.'

'What makes you think he'll bother coming after me?' she asked, while wondering dizzily what the two men had quarrelled about.

'Everyone knows he'd die for you,' Freddy raged. 'I'm not blind or deaf, neither are other people!'

'You're mistaken, I'm afraid.' Zoe wiped sadly the sea-spray from her eyes.

'You're the one who's mistaken, darling! If you don't believe me just take a look behind you,' he replied.

It was Reece. As she turned, Zoe was praying instinctively that it wouldn't be, but it was. He was in one of the powerboats from the yard and he appeared to have Ian with him. Zoe stared, feeling cold with apprehension. He was coming up fast, for he had skills when it came to this kind of thing which Freddy Vintis knew nothing about. For him there would be nothing out of the ordinary in rescuing his foolish young wife from the irresponsible clutches of another man, but suddenly she dreaded his anger.

Then her terrified gaze was torn abruptly in the other direction as Freddy suddenly clutched her arm. He hadn't noticed a large ferry approaching, and they were directly in its path. 'Oh, my God!' he began shouting, over and over again.

That they avoided it seemed nothing short of a miracle. Zoe was barely conscious of thrusting a shaking, useless Freddy out of the way and grabbing the wheel, then acting automatically as Reece would have done. As she had done on the night they had been lost in the storm. But, once the ferry was past, she was ready to admit that she and Freddy might still be both alive more because of good luck than good management. She had received a light knock on the face, but this was all.

'You fool!' she cried, now having strangely lost any desire to die. 'What on earth were you trying to do?'

'I told you,' he muttered sullenly, 'I wanted revenge. But not that way, though. I didn't see the damned thing until it was nearly on top of us!'

'You might have had your revenge, but you wouldn't have known about it,' she pointed out wryly.

'You don't have to rub it in,' Freddy snarled, taking the wheel again and to her relief turning to make for the harbour. 'I've had about enough,' he grumbled, ignoring Reece, who had come alongside. 'At least,' he added querulously, 'I've managed to teach your husband something of a lesson. He looks as if he's received a bit of a shock. He might think twice about attacking me in future!'

Zoe tried to look at Reece, but couldn't. She was aware of his boat staying dangerously close but felt too shaken to raise her eyes. She was conscious that she and Freddy must appear to have acted outrageously and that Reece might well be justified in thinking the blow on the head she had got was no more than she deserved. There was little doubt in her mind that once he had her back home, she'd be smarting in other places as well.

The bump on her face was bleeding. She could feel the blood on her skin and raised her fingers to rub it away. A cut above her eye, she guessed, where she had caught herself on a cleat as the boat rolled over out the way of the ferry. Her face felt a mess, but it probably looked worse than it was. It didn't worry her half as much as her apparent inability to stop shaking. Try as she might, she seemed to have no control over her limbs.

Freddy, with a daring boldness which amazed her, swung the boat straight into the boatyard, ignoring the harbour farther on. As he almost crashed into the jetty, Reece was there beside him, with Ian dropping a line over a piling. Even then she didn't dare look at him, not wanting to see the fury in his face, but she felt it in his hands as he reached over and hauled her bodily out of Freddy's boat.

After a swift, teeth-snapping glance at her, which appeared to do nothing to lessen his fury, he lifted her in his arms, passing her up to Donald, whose face was almost as pale as his own. 'Hold her for me, Donald,' he said, his voice like steel as he leapt up behind her and turned to confront Freddy Vintis on the wooden jetty.

'Whatever made you go with him?' Donald held Zoe anxiously, but his voice reproached her. 'The boss nearly went out of his mind!'

On Freddy's face was the smug smile of a man enjoying a joke very much in his favour. 'I brought your wife back, Macadam,' he leered. 'I'm sorry she doesn't look so pretty, but I thought you wouldn't want half the town to see, so I brought her back here.'

He got no farther. Zoe, unable to bear his expression of insolent triumph, closed her eyes. He had infuriated Reece and was making no pretence that he hadn't got a lot of pleasure out of it. It was her fault and she felt she could have died with misery. With a hopeless sob she shrank closer to the comfort of Donald's fatherly arms.

Then she heard a loud crack, a fist contacting a jaw-bone, followed by a huge splash. Startled, her eyes shot open. Freddy was floundering in the water, coming to the surface spluttering and holding a bleeding chin, while Reece stood watching, so obviously in the grip of a livid anger that no one dared speak.

'If anyone helps that bastard out of there,' he snapped to the men behind him, 'he'll suffer the same fate!' Then, as Freddy dragged himself upright, on to the jetty, muttering obscene threats, Reece hit him, again and again.

The terrible tension gripping Zoe's limbs was suddenly released. Fiercely she tried to free herself from Donald's arms. 'Stop it, Reece!' she screamed, and when he didn't she turned wildly to the unmoving circle of men. 'You have to do something!' she cried desperately. 'Don't encourage him. He'll murder him!'

'I'd like to,' Reece snarled, 'I'd like to very much, but I think he's had enough.' As Freddy slumped to his knees, then collapsed on his face, Reece added, with what Zoe thought was brutal satisfaction, 'That's something you shouldn't forget in a hurry.'

Marvelling dazedly at the fundamental savagery of men, Zoe felt her knees begin to give again and the day begin to darken. She felt so terrible she couldn't speak, despite the way in which the men turned contemptuously from Freddy Vintis and began fussing tenderly over her.

'Come on, Zoe.' Reece shouldered his way through them to take her from Donald and pick her up. His face was still hard and set, but his voice was much more gentle. 'I think it's time I took you home.'

Clinging to him weakly, she hid her face against broad chest as with a brief word of thanks to his men he carried her to the car. As they left the yard she brushed her hair from her sore face and made an effort to pull herself together. 'I'm sorry, Reece,' she whispered, 'I wish this had never happened. What can everyone be thinking? You shouldn't have hit him.'

Reece listened to her disjointed sentences, his mouth tightened grimly. 'He deserved all he got, but don't talk now. You've had a shock and you're suffering. We both are,' he surprised her by adding tersely.

Zoe was near to tears, but found she couldn't stop talking. 'The trouble you went to settle—is it all over? Shouldn't you have stayed?'

'It was over long before you went out with Vintis,' he said repressively. 'If I'd followed my inclinations and gone straight to your grandparents' house, you might never have seen him.'

'How did you know where to find me?' she asked. 'You were right behind us.'

'Ursula rang from the harbour, or thereabouts, I believe. She told me where you'd gone. I'd actually seen Vintis pass before I answered the phone, but didn't realise you were with him.'

'The ferry was awful . . .' terror returned to her eyes as she remembered it. 'I don't know how we missed it.'

'Don't talk about it,' Reece commanded curtly, his face whitening as he drove up to the house and stopped in front of the door.

Going around to her side, he helped her out and as she swayed, picked her up again, carrying her straight upstairs to his room. Putting her carefully down on the edge of the bed, he said formidably, 'Don't move. You're shocked and hurt and I'm going to run you a bath. Then we'll talk, but not before.'

'Your hands, Reece!' for the first time Zoe saw his bleeding knuckles and was horrified.

'Don't worry,' he shrugged, 'I'm sure Vintis will be hurting much more.' He crossed the passage to the bathroom and turned on the taps. Then he came back for her and helped her undress. As she slid thankfully under the warm, soothing water, her mind was still in such a turmoil she scarcely realised what he was doing.

'I'm going down to make you a hot drink,' Reece frowned, watching her closely and anxiously, 'then I'll see to your face. I shan't be long.'

While the warmth of the water relaxed her, Zoe found it almost impossible to stay there. There was too much on her mind and it made her restless. Reece was obviously concerned, but that didn't mean he loved her. More than likely, he was merely trying to strengthen her, to give her enough courage to hear what he had to tell her without breaking down. Men became embarrassed by tears if they thought they were the cause of them.

She was out of the bath and wrapped completely in a huge, thick towel by the time he returned.

'That was too quick,' was all he said, but there seemed to be disapproval in his eyes as he took her arm and gently guided her back to his room again. After making her resume her seat on the edge of the bed, he poured her a cup of tea, liberally laced with brandy.

'It's not the right time of day for a bath,' she stammered, as his ensuing silence seemed to reproach her.

She must have been wrong in thinking he was annoyed that she hadn't stayed longer in her bath, for his dark brows merely rose indifferently. 'You were soaked and the sea is still cold, but as long as you feel better that's all that matters. The time of day is surely immaterial?'

Drinking the tea he gave her slowly, Zoe glanced at him uncertainly under lowered lashes. 'Where's yours?' she asked, wishing she knew exactly what he was thinking. 'Or are you having something stronger?'

'I've already had a drink,' he admitted, 'while I was waiting for the kettle to boil. Before I have anything more I want a look at you. That cut on your face looks as if it could do with some attention.'

'It's nothing,' she protested, 'merely a slight cut, a scratch on my brow.'

'I'm going to see to it, anyway,' Reece insisted grimly, sitting down beside her. 'You made a big enough fuss when I got a bang on the head. Now it's my turn.'

Zoe sat meekly enduring as he made a thorough examination before applying a soothing ointment to the broken skin. Why, she wondered, with a kind of quiet desperation, were they sitting here talking to each other like two strangers? His face was devoid of expression and her throat felt dried up.

'It's only superficial,' the lines on his face eased with relief, 'but I expect you're feeling sore?'

'A bit, not much. I think the tea's helping.'

He finished the dressing, then suddenly surprised her by placing his hands on her shoulders, as though his restraint had abruptly ended. Closely he gazed at her tear-stained face. 'You were crying in your bath, Zoe. I looked in, but you didn't see me. Was it just shock, reaction, or was there something else?'

Acutely miserable, she shook her head without replying. He must have come so quietly to the bathroom she hadn't heard him. She would have made more effort to stem her tears if she had known he was there.

He continued to watch her narrowly. 'What did Ursula say to make you go off as you did with a greenhorn like Vintis? It must have been something pretty drastic.'

'It was nothing,' she murmured evasively, every bit of her crying out against the discussion which must inevitably follow if she told him.

'Zoe!'

His voice warned her he wouldn't be put off, and she glanced at him despairingly. There seemed no escape. Licking dry lips, she said dully, 'She didn't tell me anything I didn't already know, so you don't have to be angry with her. She said you were going to divorce me and marry her, and that she knew you'd been—obliged, I think she said, to marry me in the first place. I felt so dreadful that when Freddy more or less whistled from his boat and asked me out, it didn't seem to matter what I did.'

'And you believed her?'

'What else could I do?' She raised eyes dark with anguish. 'We both know the truth. You never wanted to marry me. You felt you had to, but at least you never pretended to love me.'

'Oh, Zoe, my darling girl!' Suddenly, with hands that shook, Reece drew her closer, holding her glossy head fast against his shoulder. 'Had you no idea? Didn't you know I've loved you for years?'

She couldn't believe she was hearing properly. 'No,' she cried brokenly, the tension in her so great it became unbearable, 'I can't believe it.'

'I think you might be the only one who can't,' he mocked with self-derision, lifting her chin until her eyes locked with his, and amazingly, miraculously she was forced to. His eyes were yearningly alive, expressing a passion that threatened to overwhelm her. The blue of his pupils was almost black and tiny flames flickered in the depth of them. She had a heady sensation of looking into his very soul and seeing her image impinged there for all time. In his eyes she read a promise of everlasting devotion.

'Why didn't you tell me?' she exclaimed at last, feeling utterly shaken. 'I love you so much I didn't know if I wanted to live when I thought I'd lost you.'

Her eyes were now as frankly revealing as his, and as if suddenly as overcome by emotion as she was he bent his head and kissed her. As his mouth covered hers, her arms went round him in a frenzy of longing and her body pressed closer. The exploration of his mouth deepened and pleasure invaded her so convulsively it began an urgent quivering inside her.

He was muttering thickly against her lips, his tone indicative that his control on his own passion was extremely limited. 'I love you,' he said, 'I want you. You don't know how much.'

The way she was responding, Zoe realised, must be an open invitation, driving him to the brink of madness. Reece's voice deepened while his hands visibly shook with the effort it took to put her a little way from him. 'We must talk first, Zoe. Let me speak, I have to explain.'

'Nothing seems to matter except that you love me,' she protested, her dazed eyes fixed on him entreatingly.

'Yes, it does.' His voice held a remembered sternness, even if it was only fleeting. 'Listen to me,' he drew a deep breath. 'I think you were about seventeen when I first realised the casual affection I'd always felt for you was changing. I wanted to know you better. I wanted you to get to know me. It was then that I went to your grandfather and told him frankly how I felt and asked his permission to take you out occasionally.'

'You did?' Her green eyes widened in bewilderment as he paused. 'I never guessed . . .'

'Yes,' his mouth tightened, 'but when I told your grandfather I had marriage very much in mind, he said you were too young and asked me to wait until you were twenty. He considered the difference in our ages too great and insisted I might easily sweep you off your feet, if I persisted, without giving you a chance to get to know boys of your own age.'

'And you agreed?' Zoe frowned.

'I know I like my own way,' he smiled slightly at her widening eyes, 'but I did see his point of view. It wasn't going to be easy, though, if you were around all the time. That was why I refused to have you as my secretary, and when I did give in why I went out now and again with other women. It was a kind of self-protection, as once you were back I realised I loved you as much as ever.'

'Yet you still never said anything?' she whispered incredulously.

'No, because your grandfather was still begging me to wait, but after you were nineteen I'm afraid I refused to listen. I only promised not to rush you, but afterwards I considered that a huge joke. You were so prickly I couldn't get near you. I seemed to be getting precisely nowhere.'

'I thought you were only amusing yourself with me.' Stunned by such revelations, Zoe paled. 'And I didn't realise I loved you until the night of the storm. Even then I fought it.'

'And me!' Reece kissed her briefly, a blissful kind of punishment. 'I nearly made you mine on Sam Colter's island. The irony of it was, I didn't want to do anything that might make you feel you had to marry me, and you'll never know what it cost me to take my hands off you. You were out of control and so was I—almost, my love.'

'Then we returned and my grandfather made you . . .'

'No, he didn't,' Reece interrupted dryly. 'He was convinced I'd deliberately flouted his wishes. Remember I'd already done so by telling him I would wait no longer. He thought I'd deliberately seduced you so he would have no other option but to give his permission for our marriage, while I, to my shame, thought it too good an opportunity to miss. You see, darling, on the island I recognised that we had something between us not given to everyone. You've no idea how you tempted me that night, but I was more than glad, when we returned, that I hadn't possessed you, or you would have felt doubly trapped.'

'I believed it was you who was trapped,' she exclaimed, 'and I didn't know what to think when you rushed off next day to Edinburgh.'

'I had to make sure of you,' he trailed gentle fingers down her cheek, 'and seeing my parents and making a public announcement seemed the best way of doing it. I'm sorry, darling,' he added thickly.

'You don't look it particularly,' Zoe commented, her mouth quivering unhappily as she recalled the heartache she had suffered.

'All the same I shouldn't have acted so high-handedly,' he insisted.

'I couldn't understand why you were in such a hurry.' Pain crept into her voice. 'I thought you loved Ursula.'

'Never,' he replied grimly. 'I've never loved another woman but you, or pretended to. What she said about a divorce was pure fabrication and I'm sure no one else will listen to her vindictive tales. I took her out mostly because she asked me to and I was trying to make you jealous. As I was jealous of Ian Graham and Freddy Vintis, I'm afraid,' he added ruefully.

'I'm sorry about Freddy Vintis,' Zoe said carefully, 'but I still think you were a little hard on him.'

'That's because you don't know the whole story, my child, but even if he had only been guilty of running off with you, as he did, it would have been enough.'

Zoe felt and looked and looked puzzled. 'What is the whole story, then?'

Reece sighed, finding no pleasure in relating it. 'He was the cause of all the trouble at the yard. While I've been away he's been there every day raging at the men over the boats we were building for him until they were ready to walk out. I'd just got them calmed down when he arrived this morning, and I put up with as much sheer insolence as I could stand before asking him politely—more politely than I felt, I can tell you, to remove himself and his order elsewhere. I got in touch with his father and apparently they're going back to London; coming here hasn't worked out. He apologised for his son and I was just beginning to feel slightly better when Ursula rang and said where you were. To say I was mad would be putting it mildly, but oh, God, darling,' he crushed her to him, his eyes completely black, 'when I saw that ferry bearing down on you if I could have got my hands on Vintis then I would have killed him!'

'Later you almost did,' she reminded him.

'Yes, and I'd do it again and make a better job of it this time,' he assured her, with such curt relish she shivered. 'Let's forget about him, though,' his glance went longingly over her. 'While I can still think straight I want to explain about our honeymoon. I took you to Mexico City because I thought, by combining a little business with seeing my friends, I would be able to keep our marriage on a purely friendly basis until you got used to it. Unfortunately it didn't work out quite like that, although I did my best to be guilty of only one lapse, but I wished afterwards with all my heart that I'd been more gentle.'

'I was only unhappy,' Zoe confessed, blushing crimson, 'because you didn't sleep with me again.'

'Ah, was that what was wrong, my love?' His mouth quirked in sudden amusement, while his eyes gleamed wickedly on her hot cheeks and towel-clad body. 'Well, I promise I'm going to make up for lost time,' his voice deepened in a threatening nature. 'You're my wife and I love you and want you, but I must warn you,' he teased softly, 'those nightdresses your grandmother gave you, she'll be saying in five years' time how well they've worn, because you might never have them on.'

Zoe giggled, beginning to feel strangely lightheaded as desire flared in Reece's eyes. He teased, but that was only on the surface. Underneath she recognised his need-roughened emotions, the slaking of which promised ecstasy. She let her hands slide to his shoulders, trying not to notice how he was deftly removing her towel. As air touched her smooth body she shivered, but it was only momentarily.

'Darling,' she murmured daringly, her heart beating frantically, 'if a bath is permissible in the middle of the day, do you think . . .?'

She got no further. With a huskily drawn breath Reece bent her back to the bed, kissing her deeply until she responded with a passion which clearly revealed the depth of her feelings. 'Say you love me,' he demanded fiercely against her mouth.

'I love you.' Startled from the pleasure she found in obeying him, she tightened her arms round his neck.

'And I you. Now and always,' he replied passionately, and began kissing her again, arousing in her a dizzying, mindless rapture. 'Do I need to tell you,' he muttered thickly, 'we won't be going anywhere now, or tonight?'

Zoe raised no objections, being quite certain she only wanted one thing, and that was to stay here with Reece for ever. With a contented sigh she snuggled closer and agreed. Outside the wind increased and a sudden storm blew up, but this time neither of them so much as heard it.

Harlequin® Plus

A WORD ABOUT THE AUTHOR

Margaret Pargeter was born in the quiet Northumbrian Valley, in the extreme northeast of England, where she lives today.

When did she first feel an urge to write? "Truthfully, I can't recall," she admits. "It must have been during my early teens. I remember carrying a notebook in my pocket, and while milking cows I would often take a break to scribble something down."

The jottings developed into short stories, and Margaret's first break came several years after she had married. Her husband talked her into entering a writing contest, and her work caught the eye of an editor, who asked her to write serial stories. From there she went on to complete her first romance novel, *Winds from the Sea* (Romance #1899).

Among the author's many blessings, which she likes to keep counting, is the "pleasure I get from knowing that people enjoy reading my books. And," she adds, "I hope they long continue to do so."

Legacy of PASSION

BY CATHERINE KAY

A love story begun long ago comes full circle...

Venice, 1819: *Contessa Allegra di Rienzi, young, innocent, unhappily married.* She gave her love to Lord Byron—scandalous, irresistible English poet. Their brief, tempestuous affair left her with a shattered heart, a few poignant mementos—and a daughter he never knew about.

Boston, today: *Allegra Brent, modern, independent, restless.* She learned the secret of her great-great-great-grandmother and journeyed to Venice to find the di Rienzi heirs. There she met the handsome, cynical, blood-stirring Conte Renaldo di Rienzi, and like her ancestor before her, recklessly, hopelessly lost her heart.

Now's your chance to discover the earlier
books in this exciting series.

Choose from this list of great
SUPERROMANCES!

SUPERROMANCE

Complete and mail this coupon today!

Worldwide Reader Service

In the U.S.A.
1440 South Priest Drive
Tempe, AZ 85281

In Canada
649 Ontario Street
Stratford, Ontario N5A 6W2

Please send me the following SUPERROMANCES. I am enclosing my check or money order for $2.50 for each copy ordered, plus 75¢ to cover postage and handling.

☐ # 8	☐ # 14	☐ # 20
☐ # 9	☐ # 15	☐ # 21
☐ # 10	☐ # 16	☐ # 22
☐ # 11	☐ # 17	☐ # 23
☐ # 12	☐ # 18	☐ # 24
☐ # 13	☐ # 19	☐ # 25

Number of copies checked @ $2.50 each = $_____
N.Y. and Ariz. residents add appropriate sales tax $_____
Postage and handling $_____.75

                TOTAL $_____

I enclose _____ .
(Please send check or money order. We cannot be responsible for cash sent through the mail.)
Prices subject to change without notice.

NAME_____
                       (Please Print)
ADDRESS_____APT. NO._____
CITY_____
STATE/PROV._____
ZIP/POSTAL CODE_____

Offer expires February 28, 1983   21156000000